STAR

"Will we be happy in the Rockies, Pa?"

"I can't predict."

"I just don't want to get there and find out I hate it. It would make me so sad, I would cry."

"We'll make the best of what we find," Samuel told her. "The important thing is that we'll be free. If you have to cry, cry for joy. Cry for freedom, girl. Cry for freedom, because your life will never be the same."

"All we have to do is get there alive," Randa said.

"That's all."

"What if we don't? What if all of us are killed?"

"The important thing is the trying. And I'd rather die free than die as a slave. I'd rather hold my head high when I meet our Maker."

"Let's hope it doesn't come to that, Pa."

The Wilderness series:

#1: KING OF THE MOUNTAIN
#2: LURE OF THE WILD
#3: SAVAGE RENDEZVOUS
#4: BLOOD FURY
#5: TOMAHAWK REVENGE
#6: BLACK POWDER JUSTICE
#7: VENGEANCE TRAIL
#8: DEATH HUNT
#9: MOUNTAIN DEVIL
HAWKEN FURY (Giant Edition)
#10: BLACKFOOT MASSACRE
#11: NORTHWEST PASSAGE
#12: APACHE BLOOD
#13: MOUNTAIN MANHUNT
#14: TENDERFOOT
#15: WINTERKILL
#16: BLOOD TRUCE
#17: TRAPPER'S BLOOD
#18: MOUNTAIN CAT
#19: IRON WARRIOR
#20: WOLF PACK
#21: BLACK POWDER
#22: TRAIL'S END
#23: THE LOST VALLEY
#24: MOUNTAIN MADNESS
#25: FRONTIER MAYHEM
#26: BLOOD FEUD
#27: GOLD RAGE
#28: THE QUEST
#29: MOUNTAIN NIGHTMARE
#30: SAVAGES
#31: BLOOD KIN
#32: THE WESTWARD TIDE
#33: FANG AND CLAW
#34: TRACKDOWN
#35: FRONTIER FURY
#36: THE TEMPEST
#37: PERILS OF THE WIND
#38: MOUNTAIN MAN
#39: FIREWATER
#40: SCAR
#41: BY DUTY BOUND
#42: FLAMES OF JUSTICE
#43: VENGEANCE
#44: SHADOW REALMS
#45: IN CRUEL CLUTCHES
#46: UNTAMED COUNTRY
#47: REAP THE WHIRLWIND
#48: LORD GRIZZLY
#49: WOLVERINE
#50: PEOPLE OF THE FOREST (Giant Edition)
#51: COMANCHE MOON
#52: GLACIER TERROR
#53: THE RISING STORM
#54: PURE OF HEART
#55: INTO THE UNKNOWN
#56: IN DARKEST DEPTHS
#57: FEAR WEAVER

WILDERNESS #58:
CRY FREEDOM

David Thompson

LEISURE BOOKS  NEW YORK CITY

Dedicated to Judy, Shane, Joshua and Kyndra.

A LEISURE BOOK®

December 2008

Published by

Dorchester Publishing Co., Inc.
200 Madison Avenue
New York, NY 10016

ISBN 10: 0-8439-6094-9
ISBN 13: 978-0-8439-6094-5

Printed in the United States of America.

10 9 8 7 6 5 4 3 2 1

Wilderness #58:
Cry Freedom

Chapter One

The young man with the whip had been drinking.

It showed in his red face and swaggering stride as he came out of the gleaming whitewashed mansion and descended the marble steps. Walking under great cedars, he made for a path that would take him deep into the plantation. He shook the whip as he walked and muttered under his breath, and when one of his mother's cats came toward him, he kicked it. "I will by God teach you and I will by God teach her!"

Another young man came running and fell into step beside him. "What are you up to, Brent?"

They were enough alike in face and frame to show they were brothers. Brent was older by a few years and heavier of build. Both had the red Sullivan hair and the square Sullivan jaw. Both had eyes as blue as an Irish lake.

"Leave me be, Justin."

"Why the whip?"

"Leave me be, damn you," Brent snapped.

"Father won't like it. Father won't like it one bit."

"It's not him she did this to."

"So that's what this is about?"

The cedars gave way to the emerald Bermuda grass

of the plantation lawn. Several geese were pecking at a zinnia bed, and without breaking stride Brent lashed the whip and scattered them. "Damn birds. We'll have one for supper tomorrow."

"Please reconsider," Justin said.

Brent shot him a dark glance of annoyance. "You can be a trial, you know that? If it were anyone but you, I'd take this whip to them. By God, just see if I wouldn't."

To the north a field of cotton was being worked, the overseer and two score slaves toiling in the hot Georgia sun.

"I hate it when you get like this. That temper of yours is forever getting you into trouble."

"What I do not need," Brent declared, "is someone scolding me over my temper. You have one yourself. It comes with the blood."

Justin sighed and shook his head and kept on matching his brother's long strides. "We have a couple of minutes yet. You don't have to do this."

"I swear."

"Father doesn't like them mistreated. He won't let them be punished without his consent. But I'm not telling you anything you don't already know."

"'Father this' and 'father that,'" Brent spat. "You make him sound halfway holy. But the truth is, he doesn't like them to be beaten because they're his property and he doesn't like his property damaged."

"They are people like you and me."

Brent abruptly stopped and looked at his brother in genuine amazement. "That is the stupidest thing you've ever said to me."

"Oh, please."

"I mean it. How can you compare them to us?

We're white. They're black. They're dumb brutes, the whole lot of them, little better than animals, and good for nothing."

A red tinge crept up Justin's face. "I don't care what you or anyone else says. I have always thought of them as human beings and I always will." He paused. "If they're the brutes you claim, how is it you are so upset because one of them had the gall to say no to your advances? Surely it shouldn't matter."

"I am her master and she will damn well do as I want."

"Lust, brother. Lust."

"What about it?" Brent gestured sharply and resumed walking. "I have needs, the same as any man. And she is a beauty, that Randa. The equal of any belle we know. But if you tell any of them that, I'll deny it."

"You deny a lot of things."

"What's that supposed to mean?" Brent swore and walked faster, but his brother stayed with him. "Damn you. Damn that conscience of yours, too. I'm thankful I don't have one."

"Think of the trouble it could cause. The other slaves won't like it. They'll think it unfair and harbor resentment."

Again Brent Sullivan stopped. "There's just no end to your silliness, is there? They are *slaves*, for God's sake. Who cares what they think? They're on this earth for one purpose and one purpose only. Your problem is that you make them out to be more than they are. I sometimes wonder if you even notice their skin is different than ours."

"I'm proud to say I don't. To me all skin is the same."

"Then you're a fool, Justin," Brent said heatedly.

"How can you have lived your whole life on our plantation and not make the distinction? How can you have lived in the South all your years and not take things as they are?"

They were almost at the end of the lawn when Justin cleared his throat and said, "I have never thought it right to hold another person in bondage. And that is what we do. We put our boots to the backs of their necks and bend them to our will."

"You are a freak," Brent declared.

"Not many feel as I do, true. Not south of the Mason-Dixon Line, anyway. But that doesn't make me wrong."

"It doesn't make you right." Brent swore some more. "All this talk is clearing my head. I need more brandy." He patted his pockets. "Damn. I left my flask inside."

"Good. The last thing you need is more drink."

Brent glared. "No good can come of this attitude of yours. Slavery has been around forever and always will be. Need I remind you that in Africa there are blacks who have slaves of their own? You make us out to be wicked when we are no worse than anyone else."

"I grant you the ways of the world are twisted—" Justin began.

"Enough. I'll hear no more. I started out hot and I will stay hot. Take yourself and your 'all men are equal' tripe and go bother someone else."

The shacks appeared, row after row. Most of the men and many of the women were out in the fields. Children stopped playing to stare. A crone's brow wrinkled in worry.

"Please don't do this," Justin tried again.

"Go away, I say." Brent stopped in front of the

next shack and placed his hands on his hips. From within came soft humming. "Randa! Come on out here, girl!"

The humming stopped and a middle-aged woman in a plain dress and apron, her hands caked with flour, timidly emerged. "Master Brent, Master Justin." Her wide eyes focused on the whip. "What can I do for you?"

"Emala, I want your daughter, and I want her now."

Emala wiped her hands on her apron.

"Didn't you hear me?"

"Randa ain't here, Master Brent. She's off with the rest and won't be back 'til sunset." Emala's throat bobbed. "If you don't mind my askin', what's this about? You sound awful mad."

"I am. That daughter of yours has overstepped herself and must be taught a lesson."

"With that, Master Brent?" Emala asked with a fearful nod at the whip. "What could she have done that's so bad?"

"Hasn't she told you?" Brent glowered at the shack. "Are you sure she's not hiding in there and you're not lying to protect her?"

"I'd never do that, Master Brent, sir."

"We'll see." Brent barreled on in. The bare walls, the burlap curtains, the sparse furnishings were typical. He snorted and came back out. Squinting up at the morning sun, he swore bitterly. "I want you to tell her something for me, Emala."

"I surely will, Master Brent."

"Tell her I did not take kindly to last night. I did not take kindly at all to what she did. She should be flattered. She should think of the good it can do her and your family."

Emala wrung her hands, her knuckles pale against the ebony. "I will tell her, Master Brent."

"See that you do."

Justin watched his brother stalk off. "I'm sorry, Emala. You know how he gets. He came home late and was drinking until nearly dawn."

Fixing her big brown eyes on him, Emala said, "I like you, Master Justin. I like you a lot. You're the nicest white man I ever knew, and that's a fact. So I hope you won't hold it against me when I say I'm scared of your brother. Powerful scared. I remember when he whipped old Gus for droppin' that plate."

"I was in Atlanta with father or we would have stopped him. And father did take away his stable privileges for a month, if you'll recall."

"His stable privileges," Emala said.

Justin gazed out over the plantation. "It's a strange world we've been born into, isn't it? I sometimes wish I was a Quaker. They are against slavery, you know. And Denmark has outlawed it."

"Denmark, sir? I ain't never heard of that town."

"It's a country on the other side of the ocean."

"It would be," Emala said.

"Mark my words. The day will come when all men, white and black, are free."

"If you say so, sir."

"Never give up hope. Tomorrow is always a better day." Justin smiled and hastened after his brother.

The moment he was out of sight, Emala turned and made a bustling beeline for a field to the south. The foreman was there, but he did not try to stop her as she went down the rows of cotton to where a large man in a tattered floppy hat was on his knees, working at the soil with his fingers. He had a bulbous nose and thick lips that curled in surprise.

"What the devil are you doin' here, woman? You have the day off. I thought you was bakin'."

"We got trouble, Samuel."

Samuel came off his knees, rising until he towered over her. His sleeveless shirt was damp with sweat, and the corded muscles on his arms rippled as he moved. "What kind of trouble? If it's Chickory again, I'll take a switch to that boy's backside. Just see if I don't."

"It's not Chick, it's Randa."

"You're joshin'. That girl hardly ever gives us grief. We've been lucky with her. She's not like some of the others, always triflin' with men, carryin' on and whatnot."

"It might be better for her if she was like them."

Samuel was shocked. "Wash your mouth out with lye soap. And you her own mother. Why, if you was a drinkin' woman, I'd say you'd been at the bottle."

"Master Brent has, and he's after our girl with a whip."

"What's that?"

"You heard me. He tried to take liberties last night and she wouldn't let him, so now he came to our shack with his whip and his brother."

"Hold on, hold on," Samuel said. "You're goin' too fast. What's this about liberties? How come you know about it and I don't? Why wasn't I told?"

"Because I knew how you would be. You'd want to take a club to him, and then I'd have my husband hangin' from a noose. No thank you. I made Randa promise not to say a word to you and figured that would be the end of it."

"Damn you, woman."

"Don't take that tone with me, Samuel Worth. Or have you forgotten what you did when Amos Sully was pesterin' her? You thrashed him, thrashed him good. He was black so nothin' came of it, but it ain't the same when you thrash white folks. And especially not your master. They have laws about that."

"White laws," Samuel said.

"Forget the law and forget Master Brent," Emala said. "The question now is what do we do? He went away, but he'll be back, most likely tonight after the work is done. How do we stop him? Go to Master Frederick? His father is the only one who can control him."

Samuel glanced at the other workers to be sure none were within earshot. Then, bending toward her, he said quietly, "We run."

"Samuel!"

"I'm serious, woman."

"You're sunstruck, is what you are. You know what the whites do to those who run."

Samuel looked around again, then clasped her hand. "It's not as if we haven't talked about it. Sure, Master Frederick treats us decent, but he still owns us. And I don't like bein' owned. I want to be free. To be my own man. To go where I want and do what I want when I want."

"I've told you before and I will tell you again," Emala whispered, "that kind of thinkin' can get you hurt or worse."

"And how hurt will our daughter be if Master Brent takes his whip to her?" Samuel grasped her other hand. "You have to make up your mind. Either we run, or I try to stop him. And you know what they do to blacks who stand up to whites."

Emala bit her lower lip.

"I don't care to spend the rest of my days in these fields. My father did it and his father before him, but it's not for me. I've only stuck it out this long because of you and the kids."

"Were would we go? We can't stay in the South. They'd hunt us down like they do all the runaways. We'd have to go to Yankee land and be at their mercy."

"You sound like Miss Colleen," Samuel said. "To her they are Yankees. To us they are just more whites. But no." Samuel raised his head to the west. "I have me a better idea. We'll run, all right. But we'll go the last place anyone would expect."

"Where's that?"

"The Rocky Mountains."

Chapter Two

With caution born of long experience, two riders made their way along the green belt of vegetation that fringed the winding Platte River.

The man was big and broad of shoulder. Endless hours in the sun had bronzed his features so that he might easily be mistaken for an Indian were it not for his beard and his piercing green eyes. His fringed buckskins, his possibles bag and ammo pouch and powder horn, marked him as a frontiersman. In his long hair he wore a single white feather that hung down at the back. A wide leather belt girthed his waist. Wedged under it were a pair of flintlock pistols. On his left hip hung a bowie, on his right a tomahawk.

The woman was average-sized and shapely, her soft doeskin dress decorated with blue beads. Both her hair and her eyes were dark. She also had an ammo pouch and powder horn. Two pistols were tucked under her thin belt. The bone hilt of a knife jutted a sheath on her right hip. In addition, across her saddle she held a Hawken rifle.

Wildlife teemed about them. In the thickets sparrows chirped and flitted. A robin warbled high in a tree. A startled rabbit bounded from their path. A doe and her fawn rose from their rest to prick up their long ears and then bolt in alarm.

"I do so love the Platte," Winona King said in her flawless English. A gifted linguist, she was well versed in several tongues.

Nate King grunted. "As a river it makes a great puddle."

Winona laughed merrily. The Platte wasn't much as rivers went, so shallow and narrow that she was surprised the whites hadn't named it Platte Creek. "At least it runs all year," she noted. Unlike some of the waterways in the Rockies that dried up during the summer months. "We won't die of thirst before we reach Missouri."

"We wouldn't go thirsty anyway," Nate said a trifle indignantly. He took her remark as a slight slur on his ability. If they had to, they could always mop up the morning dew with a cloth or shirt and wring out enough water to keep them alive.

"My, someone is prickly today," Winona teased.

"And you've been awful happy for days now," Nate remarked. Not that she had a sour disposition. Quite the contrary. His wife was usually cheerful and good-natured. The same could be said of most Shoshones. It stemmed in part from their outlook on life, which differed drastically from the outlook of many whites.

"I am happy," Winona admitted. "We have not had much time alone together in a good long while. And I am looking forward to visiting St. Louis again."

"I'm not," Nate grumbled. Not given the reason for their journey. Frowning, he glanced down at the rifle sheath tied to the side of his big bay. The stock of his Hawken poked from the end. His *busted* Hawken. And he without any means to repair it short of taking it to the men who had made it for him, the famed Hawken brothers of St. Louis.

"Now, now," Winona said. "It was an accident. It could have happened to anyone."

"I suppose." But Nate took little consolation in this fact. He prided himself on always being careful, on not making mistakes, and he made one the morning he went to the corral at the back of their cabin to calm their agitated horses. He'd had his rifle with him, as always, and after opening the gate, he leaned it against the rails. A mistake, as it turned out, for when he reached for one of the horses, it shied and kicked, and a flailing hoof struck the Hawken, bending the breech and cracking the stock.

"Blame the cat, not yourself," Winona said.

Nate's frown became a scowl. A mountain lion had taken to paying their cabin frequent visits. A young mountain lion, he suspected, drawn by the scent of their horses. In turn, its scent was to blame for getting the horses so worked up. It hadn't attacked the horses yet, but if things kept up, it was only a matter of time. As soon as he got back from St. Louis, he was going after it.

Winona breathed deep and asked, "Don't you love the prairie, husband?"

Nate grunted a second time. He liked the prairie just fine, but he liked the mountains more. Give him the snowcapped peaks and miles-high majesty of the Rockies any day over the vista of unending grass broken by occasional strips of woodland.

"Am I talking to myself?"

"I heard you," Nate said.

"You could have fooled me."

Nate twisted in the saddle. "I have a lot on my mind, is all." Which wasn't entirely true, but he didn't want her to think he was still in a funk over his rifle, even if he was.

"Such as?"

Nate thought fast. "Our daughter."

"Oh." Winona had been thinking about Evelyn a lot lately, too. Their little girl was no longer little. Evelyn had grown into a fine young woman, and several young men had noticed. For a while a Crow and an Ute had courted her. But now it was a young man from an Eastern tribe whose family had settled in their valley. Degamawaku was his name, or Dega as they called him, and it was obvious to everyone—except Evelyn—that Dega was very much in love with her.

"That's all you have to say?"

"What will be, will be, as you whites have it. There is little we can do. She is old enough to make her own decisions. If she picks Dega for her husband, all we can do is wish them the best."

Nate was making a habit of grunting. He liked Dega, genuinely liked him, but he wasn't entirely sure Evelyn should take up with him. He would prefer she stayed single for a few more years. He said as much.

"We can't control love, husband," Winona remarked. She was a good example. She had never expected to give her heart to a white man. She had never even entertained the thought. But along he came, those many years ago, and she had fallen deeply and hopelessly in love with him.

"I suppose," Nate begrudged her.

Winona chuckled.

"What?"

"How did you put it? As a conversationalist you make a great tree stump."

"Only you," Nate said.

"Only me what?"

"Would use the word 'conversationalist.' Most whites use ten-cent words. But you're partial to the fifty-dollar variety."

"I can't help it if whites don't know their own tongue." Truth was, Winona took great pride in her ability to learn new languages.

Despite himself, Nate grinned. Back when they first met, she'd picked up English so fast, it astounded him. It was his first inkling that his new wife was, in some respects, smarter than he would ever be. For him, learning a new tongue was like wrestling a griz. He was a plodding turtle to her hare.

Suddenly Nate stiffened. The gentle gurgling of the Platte and the singing of the birds had lulled him into briefly letting down his mental guard. He wasn't paying as much attention as he should to their surroundings. Crackling and rustling from up ahead remedied that.

Drawing rein, Nate put a hand on one of his pistols. He figured it might be more deer or maybe even elk. But then a brown silhouette appeared against the backdrop of verdant green. "No," Nate said.

The vegetation parted, framing a huge shaggy head with a shaggy mane and beard. Sickle horns glinted in the sunlight. Black nostrils flared and the creature snorted. The next instant it exploded out of the greenery.

"Buffalo!" Nate had time to cry as he reined sharply and jabbed his heels. His bay responded superbly, bounding out of the brute's path and away from its raking horns.

Winona had seen Nate stop. She could not see what he was looking at, but she did hear the snort and knew what made it. Even as he shouted his warning, she yanked on the sorrel's reins. The buffalo streaked past the bay and was on top of her in the blink of an eye. The split-second warning enabled her to evade it, but with inches to spare.

Nate drew one of his pistols, a .55-caliber smoothbore flintlock, powerful enough to bring the buff down but only if he hit it in the vitals. And that was no easy task. A thick skull protected the brain and the internal organs were encased in layers of muscle and hide. Still, he had to try. As the bull spun to come at them again, Nate took a hasty bead on a gleaming eye and fired.

At the blast the buffalo jerked its head, but it wasn't severely hurt. The lead ball had missed the eye and glanced off the thick bone that ringed it.

"Ride!" Winona urged, and goaded her sorrel into a gallop. She made for the open prairie, where her horse had a better chance of outrunning the horned behemoth.

The buffalo veered after her.

Fear coursed through Nate. The thing was almost on top of her. Another few seconds and it would slam into Winona's mount with the impact of a battering ram. He had witnessed the result before, when a Shoshone warrior failed to get out of the way of a charging bull and its raking horn ripped the warrior's horse open like a hot knife ripping through butter.

"No!" Nate cried. He rode straight at the bull, unsure if his bay would do as he wanted or break away at the last instant. The jolt of the impact nearly unhorsed him. But it had the desired effect. The bay's shoulder slammed against the buffalo's, throwing the buff off stride and causing it to stumble and nearly fall. Then Nate was past and flying in the wake of his wife's sorrel. "Keep going! Don't stop!"

Winona had started to rein around. His rash move to save her both horrified and elated her. Horror, because the bay might have gone down, leaving Nate at the buff's mercy. Elation, because of the depth of his love for her. Then there was no time to think of anything but flight; the bull was thundering after them in determined fury.

Nate caught up to her just as she reached the open prairie and they galloped side-by-side. He saw no other buffs, which was peculiar. Buffalo were nearly always in herds. A glance back explained why this one was alone. It was old, and from the way it ran, one of its front legs had been hurt at one time and hadn't mended as it should. Old and crippled, but that made it no less formidable. Six feet high at the shoulders, with a horn spread of three feet, and weighing upward of two thousand pounds, qualified it as a veritable monster.

The drum of hooves rang in Nate's ears as he lashed his reins and slapped his legs. The bay and the sorrel were neck and neck, their manes and tails flying. The buff was a good ten yards back and wasn't gaining, but it wasn't losing ground, either.

"Faster!" Winona cried, and tried to urge her sorrel to greater effort. But it was already galloping as fast as it could.

Nate had slid his spent flintlock under his belt and now drew the other one. He didn't want to shoot again if he could help it, but if the buff caught up he wouldn't have a choice. At that moment he deeply regretted not being able to use his rifle. A single well-placed shot could bring the bull down as slickly as could be.

Intent on the buffalo, Nate wasn't watching the ground in front of them. Then Winona hollered.

In their haste to escape they had blundered onto a prairie dog town. A *large* prairie dog town, covering some twenty to thirty acres. Scores upon scores of conical dirt mounds over a foot high and two feet wide dotted the prairie, all laced with entrance and exit holes large enough for a horse to step into and break its leg.

Nate's skin crawled. Under normal circumstances he wouldn't ride anywhere near a prairie dog colony. No sane rider would. At any moment he expected to hear an ominous crack and feel the bay lurch under him.

Winona saw a prairie dog rise onto its hind legs and utter a shrill whistle. Normally she regarded its kind as adorable and liked to watch their playful antics. But not now, not here. Her sorrel's front hoof came down dangerously close to a hole, and she almost cried out.

"Slow down!" Nate shouted. He didn't want to, not with the hairy engine of destruction bearing down on them. But they couldn't afford to lose either of their mounts.

Winona was going to do more than that. She had made up her mind to stop the buffalo herself. She had her rifle, and she was a good shot. She slowed and shifted, jamming the stock to her shoulder. But try as she might, she couldn't hold the rifle steady. No matter. Thumbing back the hammer, she sighted down the bouncing barrel as best she could.

Suddenly the sorrel whinnied.

Nate saw it step into a hole. His breath caught in his throat and his blood became ice. He reined to the right to try and grab Winona, but she was thrown over the sorrel's neck and hit hard on her shoulder. Panic-stricken, Nate hauled on the reins to bring his bay to a stop.

Pain filled Winona. For a few seconds she lay dazed. It didn't feel like any of her bones were broken. She was aware she had lost her rifle.

"Winona!"

A snort brought Winona out of herself, and she looked up to see the bull bearing down on her, its great head lowered to rend and tear. Fear balled her gut, but it didn't stop her from groping about for her Hawken.

The *snap* of a bone breaking was as loud as a gunshot. In a whirl of legs and tail, the buffalo crashed to the ground and slid on its side, plowing prairie dog mounds under its enormous bulk and raising a choking cloud of dust.

Winona coughed and swatted at the dust and rolled over, and suddenly she was nose to nose with one of the most formidable creatures in the wild.

The bull was trying to get back up but its broken leg wouldn't bear its weight. Down it crashed, almost on top of her. Its eyes locked on hers.

"Don't move!" Nate warned.

Winona froze. She could feel the buffalo's warm breath on her cheek. Its odor filled her nostrils.

Nate extended his pistol and once again aimed at an eye. He was close enough now that he shouldn't miss.

Then the bull rumbled deep in its barrel chest, twisted its head, and hooked a horn at Winona's face.

Chapter Three

They had to wait until dark, and for Emala the wait was awful. She rocked in her chair and gazed out the window of their shack and continually wrung her hands in despair. She also prayed, prayed with all her heart.

In less than an hour her Samuel would be back from the fields. Randa, too. Chickory was over at the small plantation sawmill and might be the last one home as sometimes they worked late.

The plantation. It was the only home, the only life, Emala knew. She was born a slave, just like her mother before her, and her mother. She never thought about living any other way because the likelihood of being set free was as distant as the stars. To her knowledge, the Sullivans never freed any of their slaves. The owners of others plantations did, but never the Sullivans. She'd heard about the ones set free through the slave grapevine.

Emala heard about runners, too. From time to time some slaves simply couldn't take it anymore. They couldn't take the long, grueling hours of toil. They couldn't take always being dirt poor. They couldn't take the overseer and his whip. But most of all, they couldn't take the fact that they belonged to someone else. They couldn't take being *owned*.

For Emala, it was all she'd ever known. For her, being a slave was the natural order of things. It was how her life was, and she accepted that she couldn't change it. The drudgery didn't affect her as deeply as it did some. She would listen to them rail against their fate and shake her head.

Emala always imagined she would grow old and die on the plantation, as her mother did. The Sullivans weren't entirely heartless; older slaves were given the easier jobs and didn't work as many hours. In that regard, Frederick Sullivan treated them with a degree of respect, much as he did his hounds.

At the thought, a slight tremble ran through her. She didn't want to run. The very notion scared her so badly, it set her heart to fluttering. Runners were always caught. Always. She couldn't think of one she knew who fled and wasn't brought back by the bounty men, or planted by them. Oh, she'd heard the rumors. Tales of slaves who *did* get away. Slaves who made it to the North and took up new lives. But she didn't believe them. They were stories, like all the other stories told around the campfires at night when the slaves got together to talk and sing and dance.

Emala never, ever entertained the idea of running. To her it was silly. Worse than silly. But Samuel had been thinking about it, and when that man made up his mind, that was that. There was no changing it. He was the most stubborn man she had ever met. But she loved him, and she would do as he wanted even when every particle of her being was against the doing.

And Emala was terrified that their daughter might be whipped. She'd never been whipped, herself, but she had seen others suffer under the lash, and it was horrible beyond measure. The pain and the blood and the suffering after were enough to provoke nightmares.

Emala would do anything to spare Randa. Her sweet, wonderful daughter was everything to her. She loved that girl with all her heart and soul, and she would as soon as have both ripped from her body than see Randa lashed and bleeding. And all because Master Brent wanted Randa and Randa refused.

Good for her, Emala thought with a smile. The work was one thing; subserving the master's lust was quite another.

A lot of the women didn't mind. Not when it meant better clothes and better food and being treated special. Some flaunted themselves for that purpose, sashaying around in front of the masters to try and get their attention.

That wasn't for Randa. She had too much pride, that girl, too much dignity. Just last night Randa had said that she would work however they made her, but she would be damned if she would let them poke her. Poking was personal. Poking was private. A woman should have the right to say who poked her and who didn't, and not be picked to poke like some prize horse picked to run in a race.

The scrape of the wooden latch brought Emala out of her reverie. She stirred and sat up as her youngest came in.

"I'm all done for the day, Ma," Chickory announced.

"That's good, child." Emala would have to stop calling him that soon. Chickory was fourteen and still had a lot of growing to do, but he was on the verge of being a man and he did not like being treated as if he was ten. "How was the sawmill?"

Chickory went to the basin and filled a tin cup with water. "I'm about worn out." He looked around. "How come you ain't cookin' supper? What are we eatin' tonight?"

"All you ever think of is your belly."

"If you were as hungry as me, you'd think of your belly, too." Chickory downed the water in several loud gulps and wiped his mouth with his sleeve. "I mean it. I'm starved."

"Come over here by me and sit. We need to talk."

"About what? I been good all this week, haven't I? I didn't get into trouble once."

"You've been doin' fine," Emala agreed. "It's not about you, Chick. It's us. All of us. We're in trouble." She told him about Randa and Master Brent, and the whip, and the decision to flee the plantation. "As soon as your sister and father show, we're leavin'."

"I can't hardly believe it."

"Try not to let it upset you," Emala said. "We'll be all right provided we keep our heads." She tried to sound more confident than she felt. "So long as we get far enough before they set the dogs on us, we can get away."

"Upset?" Chick said, and his teeth showed white in the shadows. "Ma, I'm happy as can be! I hate it here. Hate it, hate it, hate it! I'd rather be free than anything, anything at all."

"You would?" It occurred to Emala that she had never talked to the boy about it before.

"Hell, yes."

"Don't swear, child. I don't abide swearin', ever. The Lord didn't give you a mouth so you could talk filthy."

"I hear men swear all the time. Women, too."

"That is them and we are us. Swear not at all, the Bible says, and you know how I am about my Bible." It was the one possession Emala valued more than any other. Her mother had seeped her in its teachings when she was little and she had done her best to impart them to her children. Unlike many of the slaves, she could read, and she'd read to Randa and Chickory every evening from the day they were born.

"I sure do know how you are."

"You would do well to live as the Bible says to live. I have tried and tried to get that through your head, but you are willful."

"Ah, Ma." Chickory squirmed under her glare. "I do the best I can. I can't help it if that Bible stuff don't stick."

"It's not 'stuff,' it's the Word of the Lord. Love the Lord thy God, child. Love Him as you have never loved anything."

"What brought this on?"

"I'm scared," Emala confessed. "Powerful scared. We're about to cross a line and once we do there ain't no turnin' back. It'll be run or die, and I don't want any of my family dead."

Chickory placed a hand on her knee. "I'll protect you, Ma."

Emala felt her eyes moisten and turned away before she shed a tear. She must be strong, for his sake as well as hers. She changed the subject by saying, "What is keepin' your sister and father?"

At that moment Samuel entered. "Has your mother told you, boy?"

Chickory nodded.

"We're leavin' as soon as it's dark enough," Samuel

told them. "And we're only takin' what we can carry."

"That's all?" Emala said. They didn't own much, but what they had she cherished; her pots and pans, her spare dresses and the shoes she wore on the most special occasions, her shawl and her hat and her sewing bag.

"We must travel light and fast." Samuel went to the rear wall and knelt. He pried at a board until a part of it came loose. Underneath was their poke. In it was the money they had scrimped and saved over the years, all of eight dollars and forty cents. Samuel shook it and the coins jingled. "I wish we had enough for a horse."

Emala said, "I wish we had enough for four horses." With mounts they stood a chance of outrunning the hounds. Without them—she did not like to think of what might happen.

Chickory cleared his throat. "Is it true what Ma said, Pa? You aim to take us clear out west?"

"To the Rocky Mountains," Samuel said. "You've heard of them, haven't you, boy?"

"I seem to recollect I have. They're way out past the Mississippi River, which folks say is the biggest river there is."

"I don't know about that. I ain't never seen it. But you're right. It's a big one." Samuel replaced the board, came over to the table, and wearily sat.

"How will we get across it, Pa?"

"We'll worry about that when we get there." Samuel began unbuttoning his shirt.

"What I want to know," Emala said, "is why the Rockies, of all places? Pennsylvania and New York are so much closer, and people there think slavery is wrong and would gladly help us get settled."

"The North ain't safe," Samuel said. "The slave hunters can cross state lines, remember?"

"Who will Master Frederick send after us?" Chickory asked. "I hope it's not Catfish. They say he can be snake mean."

"That would be my guess. Catfish is one of the best slave hunters there is. Once he takes up a hunt, he hardly eats or sleeps until the job is done."

"The man will be huntin' us, and you almost sound like you admire him," Emala said.

"I admire any man who does his work well," Samuel responded, "and Catfish does his as well as anyone. I ain't never met the man, but I hear he never fails."

"Then why are we even botherin' to run?" Emala demanded. "If you're so all-fired sure he'll catch us, runnin' is folly."

"We're doin' it for Randa, remember? Or would you have her carry the scars from being whipped for the rest of her days?" Samuel glanced out the window. "Where is that girl, anyhow? Usually she's back by now. If we don't get her out of here soon, Master Brent is likely to show up."

"What will you do to him if he tries to hurt Sissy?" Chickory asked.

"Whatever I have to do to stop him. I expect I could break his back over my knee if it came to that."

Chickory grinned. "That I'd like to see you do, Pa."

"Hush, the both of you," Emala scolded. "Thou shalt not kill. It can't get any plainer." She stabbed a finger at her husband. "And you! Talkin' that kind of silliness. The only thing you've ever killed were boll weevils and mice."

"Land sakes, woman."

"Don't 'woman' me. If you say we must run, then

I will run, but I won't abide talk of killin'. No, sir, I won't."

"All right. Don't get your dander up any more than it is." Samuel stood and stepped to the doorway. "I only want to protect my family. Is that so bad?"

"I still think we should go to Master Frederick," Emala said. "He always treats us decent."

"The cook spread word that he's in Savannah."

Emala closed her eyes and hunched forward in her chair. She felt half sick with worry and fear. Circumstance was backing her into a corner and she didn't like it one little bit. She heard Samuel come over, and his big hand covered hers.

"We can do this."

"It's so sudden."

"Have you been listenin' to me all these years when I've said how unhappy I am? Being a slave ain't no way to be. Where does it get us? We can work our whole lives long and not be any better off than we are right now. A slave has nothin' to show for bein' a slave except the yoke of bein' one."

"We're not oxen, Samuel."

"We might as well be. That's how most whites treat us. Like we're beasts of burden. Well, I'm tired of it. I'm tired of livin' under another man's heel."

"You've been lookin' for an excuse to run and now you have one," Emala said with more than a trace of bitterness.

"Maybe I have. Maybe I have. But it wasn't me who tried to force himself on an innocent young girl. I wasn't the one who came over here today with a whip. If you have to point the finger of blame, point it at Brent Sullivan. Blame him and his hankerin' for womenfolk."

"I'm not blamin' you."

Samuel gently squeezed her fingers. "It'll be hard. I won't claim different. But once we get there we'll be free. Free, Emala! That's worth any amount of hardship."

Emala opened her eyes and fought back tears. "This is the only home I've ever known."

"I'll build you one twice as big."

"It's not the size, Samuel. It's the memories." Emala had more to say but just then Chickory called out to them from over at the window.

"Randa's comin'!"

All three of them hastened out to greet her. Emala brightened considerably at the sight of her daughter's lithe form bounding toward them with the grace and speed of a fleet-footed doe. She was dressed in a simple cotton dress, her bare feet smacking the ground in a blur.

"Why is she in such an all-fired hurry?" Chickory wondered.

"Behind her!" Samuel said.

Emala's heart leaped into her throat. For hard on her daughter's heels came a grim pursuer.

Master Brent Sullivan, his face a mask of fury, shook his whip and roared, "Stop, girl! Or by God, I'll peel your hide to the bone!"

Chapter Four

Nate King loved his wife. He loved his entire family, and always put their welfare before all else. In that, he was no different than a lot of other men. He would do anything for them, even sacrifice his life for theirs if he had to.

Such was the depth of Nate's love for Winona that when her horse went down, paralyzing fear gripped him. Fear so potent, for several seconds he was held helpless in its grip. The *snap* of the bull's leg brought him out of it. As the bull tumbled, Nate reined his bay to Winona's aid. He swooped in close, so close that the bay nearly brushed the buffalo's hide. He then did something only a superb horseman could do; Comanche-fashion, he swung over the side, thrust his heavy caliber pistol at the buff's head so that the muzzle was inches from its eye, and fired just as the bull went to bury its horn in Winona's face.

This time the lead ball did not glance off. It cored the socket, bursting the eyeball in a shower of gore, and did exactly what Nate hoped it would do. It penetrated to the brain.

The bull arced up, blood spraying from the hole, and violently thrashed in its death throes.

Winona was still not out of danger. The bull was so close, it might easily crush her or impale her. She pushed to her feet to get out of there as a flailing hoof brushed her ear.

Again Nate came to his beloved's rescue. A tug on the reins, and the bay wheeled and was at her side. Again Nate leaned down, his arm looped to catch her about the waist. Winona raised her arms to make it easier, and the next moment they were flying to safety.

Belatedly, Nate remembered where they were. On all sides rose the prairie dog cones, like a sea of miniature volcanoes. He quickly drew rein before his bay suffered the same fate as the buffalo. "Are you all right?"

Winona nodded. Her shoulder hurt where she had struck the ground when she fell, but otherwise she was unharmed. Looking into his green eyes, she said softly, "Thank you for saving me."

"It's what I'm here for," Nate responded with a grin.

Winona put her hands on his cheeks and tenderly kissed him. She let the kiss linger, and when their mouths parted, she placed her forehead against his and said, "I love you with all that I am and all that I ever will be."

"I should save you from a buff every day."

"I will get to return the favor," Winona predicted.

Nate didn't doubt it. Danger was part and parcel of their life in the wilderness. Hostile Indians. Renegade whites. Savage beasts. Accidents. Hardly a month went by that something didn't happen.

"You can put me down now. I must see to my horse."

Nate reined the bay around. The bull had stopped

thrashing and now lay on its side. It was still save for the rippling of its hide. As they drew near it exhaled one last time, as loud as a bellows, and gave up whatever ghosts buffalo had to give.

The sorrel was on its feet. It hadn't moved this whole while, but stood there trembling, shaken by its spill and the proximity of the bull.

Lowering Winona, Nate climbed down. He dreaded what they would find. If the sorrel had to be put down, they would have to ride double until he could obtain another mount. He had enough money in his poke to buy one but not enough to buy one *and* have his rifle fixed, and he dearly needed his rifle fixed.

"There, there," Winona said to calm her animal. She patted its neck, then squatted and ran her hands down each of its legs. To her immense relief, none were broken. "We were lucky."

"Thank God."

Before leaving, Nate drew his bowie and set to work. He cut off the bull's tongue and gave it to Winona to wrap in a strip of buckskin and put in a parfleche. He also cut out the heart. It took some work, but it was worth the effort. "Heart and tongue," he said as he held the still warm and dripping organ in his palm. "We'll eat well tonight."

Instead of riding out of the prairie dog town, they walked, leading their horses by the reins. Now and then a little head would pop out of a hole and whistle shrilly or give a sharp squeak of indignation.

"Uppity runts."

"In a way they saved my life," Winona said.

"After almost causing you to lose it."

They rode until near twilight. Winona was unusually quiet. Nate attributed it to her harrowing experience and kept a close watch on her. Toward twilight she came out of herself, smiled at him, and said, "I would not object if we stopped a little early tonight."

"Don't mind if we do," Nate said.

The woods that fringed the Platte were alive with the chorus of birds but otherwise peaceful. Nate chose a clear spot near the water's edge and told Winona to rest while he gathered firewood and kindled a fire. He filled their coffeepot and soon had coffee on to brew. Then he brought out the pan and prepared to cook their supper.

Winona sat with her knees tucked to her chest and her arms wrapped around her legs, contemplating the crackling flames. "I have been thinking," she broke her silence.

"Uh-oh. What about?"

"Luck."

"You're talking about the bull?"

"I am talking about life. How much of it is luck. How much of what happens and what we do depends on nothing but luck. We would have died many times over had we not had a great deal of luck in our lives."

"Some would call it the hand of Providence."

"By that you mean God?" Winona asked. To her people, the Great Mystery was exactly that, and did not take the paternal hand in human affairs the whites maintained their God did. "It implies we are somehow special."

"A lot of folks believe God watches over each and every one of us. He even assigns guardian angels to see that we don't come to harm."

Winona thought of all the people she knew of, both red and white, who had died horrible deaths or suffered the most terrible agonies. Her own father and mother had been killed in a fierce fight with Blackfeet. "Those angels must take a lot of time off from their work."

"I'm only saying. I don't have all the answers." Nate began slicing strips from the heart and the tongue and laying them out in the pan.

"Neither do I, husband." Winona gazed up through the canopy of trees at the bright blue sky. "There is so much we do not really know."

Nate shrugged. "Whether it was luck or it was Providence, the important thing is you are still alive."

"You are sweet, do you know that?"

Nate said, half in jest, "Don't tell anyone. We white men like to keep things like that a secret."

"I have noticed that some whites hide their feelings from one another. Husbands do not tell their wives they love them. Wives do not show much affection to their men. Why is that?"

"Some hearts are colder than others."

"That is all there is to it? Among the Shoshones, the greatest warrior is the one with the warmest heart. Counting coup is important, but even more important is the compassion a warrior shows for his people."

"Some whites regard compassion as a weakness."

"But your Bible says to love one another? Is that not right?"

"What the Bible teaches and what people do are not always the same. For starters, not every white believes in it. And even a lot of those who do, don't practice what it preaches. Quite a few haven't even read it all the way through, but say they believe in it anyway."

Winona grinned. "Have I ever mentioned how strange whites are?"

Chuckling, Nate held the pan to the flames. The aroma filled the clearing, making his stomach growl. They hadn't eaten since sunup, and then he only had a couple of cups of coffee and a handful of pemmican.

"Are you happy, husband?"

Nate was so startled by the question, he nearly dropped the pan. "My God. Where did that come from?"

"You are, yes?"

"Winona King, that is the silliest thing you have ever asked me. Why on earth would you even bring it up?" Nate couldn't recall her ever doing so, not in all the years they had been married.

"I was talking to Blue Water Woman the other day."

"Uh-oh," Nate said again. Blue Water Woman was the Flathead wife of his best friend, Shakespeare McNair, and McNair had a knack for saying things that got him into trouble with Winona. Like the time Nate told Shakespeare that he wished Winona didn't snore so loud, and Shakespeare went and told Blue Water Woman who then told Winona. Or the time Nate casually mentioned that Winona had been a grump that morning and Shakespeare said something to Blue Water Woman, who in turn gave Winona the impression that Nate thought she was always moody.

"Be at ease. It was not about you. She was saying how she never knew true happiness until she married Shakespeare."

"They make a good couple," Nate said. Blue Water Woman had to be the most patient woman alive to put up with McNair's antics.

"It got me to thinking about us," Winona said.

"And how happy I have been as your woman. I do not regret a single day we have spent together."

"Neither do I." In fact, Nate rated marrying her as the single smartest thing he had ever done. Sure, she had what might be called quirks. Every person did. But overall she was as fine a woman and as good a wife as any man could hope for. He was about to tell her that when both the bay and the sorrel raised their heads and pricked their ears. They stared to the north, across the Platte River. Nate looked, and swore.

A grizzly stood on the other side, atop a grassy bank. Its head was raised and it appeared to be sniffing the air.

Nate could guess why. Even though there was hardly any wind, and what wind there was blew toward them, the grizzly's extremely sensitive nose had caught the faint scent of the simmering heart and tongue. "Damn. Just what we need."

Winona put a hand on her rifle. "Do you think it will cross?" She hoped not. The silver-tipped bears were notoriously hard to kill and had few rivals in sheer brute savagery.

"If it starts across we have a fast decision to make."

Winona understood. Should they stay and fight, or flee? "We haven't stripped the horses yet. We can get away before the bear reaches us."

Nate thought it wise to avoid a clash, but part of him balked at running. The part of him that in his younger years had earned him the Indian name of Grizzly Killer. Suddenly setting the pan down, he stood and strode to the river's edge. Sometimes a griz would run off at the sight of a human.

Not this one. It spotted him instantly and rose onto its hind legs for a better look.

Winona grabbed her rifle and hurried to her husband's side. "What are you up to?" It was unlike him to be so reckless.

"I'm not of a mind to leave." So saying, Nate drew a pistol and thumbed back the hammer.

"Surely you are not thinking of shooting it?"

"Surely I'm not," Nate answered, and taking aim, he fired into the river a few feet in front of the bear. A small geyser erupted, spraying drops in all directions.

For some grizzlies, that was enough to drive them off. Most bears disliked loud noises. Most would do as this one did, namely, drop onto all fours, whirl, and lope off into the woods.

Nate watched until it was lost from view. "Good riddance," he said, and grinned. "That worked out right fine, if I do say so myself."

"More of that luck," Winona said.

"Or more Providence." Nate hooked his elbow in hers and they strolled back to the fire. "First the buff, then the griz. Now all we need is a war party of hostiles to make our day complete."

"Do not joke about a thing like that," Winona cautioned, "or it might come true."

"Be careful what you wish for."

"Pardon?"

"A white figure of speech." Nate glanced over his shoulder to be sure the grizzly hadn't doubled back. They did that sometimes, with fatal consequences for those they took unawares.

Their meat was done. Nate and Winona ate right from the pan, spearing the strips with the tips of their knives. They smiled at one another, content and at ease.

"I had forgotten how much fun it is when it is just the two of us," Winona said.

"We should do this more often," Nate suggested. Now that their son, Zach, was married and had a cabin of his own, and their daughter, Evelyn, was more than old enough to take care of herself, it would be a delight to get away for a while now and then, to forget all their cares and responsibilities and just enjoy each other's company.

"How about if next month we ride up to see the glacier?"

Nate had long wanted to. The valley they lived in, deep in the heart of the mountains, got much of its water from runoff, and much of the runoff from a glacier high atop a craggy peak. "Why not?"

Winona forked a piece of heart into her mouth. The flavor had always appealed to her, and she chewed with relish.

"You know—" Nate began. He was about to say that it was too bad moments like this couldn't last forever. But Winona suddenly stiffened, and her eyes grew wide with alarm.

A growl told Nate why even before he turned. He hoped against hope he was wrong but he wasn't.

The grizzly was lumbering up out of the Platte River toward them.

Chapter Five

Randa Worth ran like the wind. She had always been fast on her feet. And she'd always loved to run for the sheer fun of it, to have the earth flash by and feel the air on her face. She often took part in races with other children, and she nearly always won.

Now her speed was being put to the test. All Randa could think of was reaching her family. She was so scared, her belly was a knot of pain. Nothing like this had ever happened to her before. To think that a man—a white man, no less, and a master of the plantation—wanted her, wanted her *that* way, shocked her more than anything, ever.

Boys had always liked her. Like all the girls, she had played with them, swam in the creek with them, did all the things girls and boys did for fun, and never, ever had cause to give any thought to *that*. It was only recently that the boys started to take notice of her in a new way. "You are blossomin' into a woman," her mother told her, and Randa wasn't so sure she wanted to. Not if all some boys wanted to do was touch her.

Then Master Brent himself took notice.

Randa was shocked when he came up to her in the field the week before last and started talking to her.

Just up and talked about the weather and the cotton and other things as if they were the best of friends, when in truth, neither he nor any of the other whites had spoken ten words to her since she was born. Except Master Frederick. He always greeted everyone warmly, and according to her mother, was the best master anyone could have.

But Master Brent was nothing like his father. He wore a perpetual scowl, as if scorning the world and everyone in it. And he hardly ever had a warm word for the slaves who worked his land. If he talked to them at all, it was to snap at them for not doing their work right or to scold them for being lazy. He also liked to use his whip.

Randa had heard rumors about something else he liked. About how he would pay black girls visits in the dark of night. Some of the girls didn't mind; some even liked it. But those who didn't had to do *that* whether they wanted to or not. The stories had scared her, but since it always happened to older girls, and since Master Brent hardly ever looked in her direction, she figured it wouldn't happen to her.

She was wrong.

The night before, Randa had been with several of her friends, talking quietly by a fire, when Master Brent appeared out of nowhere, took her by the elbow, and said they should go for a walk. Speechless with fright, Randa rose and let him lead her into the trees. He said things, words she barely caught, having to do with the moon and the cool night air and didn't she look fine in her cotton dress. And then he had pressed her against a cedar and touched her.

Randa had smelled the liquor on his breath. His nearness, his touch, turned her fear to anger. *How dare he do that to her*. How dare he take liberties without her wanting him to. She had pushed him away, but he came at her again, grinning as if they were playing at some sort of game. But it was no game to her. And when he touched her anew, Randa did the unthinkable; she slapped him, hard.

Master Brent had stepped back in surprise. He wasn't mad, not yet, but he told her not to do that again, and reached for her.

Randa was wiry, but she was strong. She'd balled her fist and struck at him but he was tight against her and she couldn't land a blow where it would really hurt. His fingers had fumbled at her dress. In a panic, she did the only thing she could think to do. She drove her knee up between his legs.

That did it. Master Brent tottered back, clutching himself and sputtering, and fell to his knees.

"Leave me be!" Randa had said, jabbing a finger at his face, and ran off. She half feared he would follow her home, but he didn't.

Her mother had been sitting on the steps to their shack, and right away she sensed something was wrong. Randa broke down in her arms and told her. But quietly, so as not to wake up her father.

They both hoped that was the end of it. Her mother said that if Master Brent bothered her again, she would go to Master Frederick. Randa had wiped the tears from her cheeks with her sleeve and gone in to sleep. She prayed that all would be well and asked God to watch over her, then pulled the blanket to her chin, curled into a ball, and quietly wept until she drifted off.

All day Randa had lived in dread of the coming night. All day she kept looking for Master Brent to show up, but he never did. The sun was dipping to the horizon when the foreman called out that they could quit for the day, and she was almost to the end of the field when a shadow fell over her and a rough hand clamped on her wrist.

"We have unfinished business, you and me," Master Brent growled. This time he had his whip with him, and he shook it, adding, "And if you act up like you did last night, you will suffer the consequences."

Fear rooted her, but only until Master Brent started to pull her toward a patch of woods. Then Randa's anger returned, hotter than ever, and she broke free and pushed him and ran.

He came after her.

Randa flew. And now all she could think of was reaching her parents. They would help her. They would not let Master Brent do what he wanted to do. When she came in sight of their shack, she poured on an extra burst of speed. She saw them come out, and relief coursed through her. Relief that was short-lived, for the next moment iron fingers seized her arm and a foot hooked her ankle and she was thrown brutally to the ground.

Randa's head swam. She blinked up into a face twisted with rage.

Master Brent gripped her by the hair and shook her. "Bitch, you are in for it now."

"Please," Randa gasped. She pushed at his arm, but he was too strong. "I never did you no harm."

"What does that have to do with anything?" Brent demanded. Suddenly stepping back, he uncoiled his whip with a flick of his wrist.

"No!" Randa pleaded, thrusting out a hand to ward off the blow. "You wouldn't."

Brent Sullivan laughed. "You are the stupidest darkie I ever met. I *own* you, you cow. I have the right to do whatever I want with you. Make love to you if I want. *Beat* you if I want." He drew back his arm.

Randa cringed. She had seen a man whipped once, and it had been horrible. The sickening sound the lash made as it tore the skin, the hideous shrieks and wails. She'd heard that a whip could flay a person's flesh down to the bone. It could easily take out an eye or rip off an ear. "Please, Master Brent!"

"Beg some more. I like it when they beg."

And then someone was between them. Legs planted firm, looming like a pillar of solid rock, Samuel Worth shook his head and said quietly, "I can't let you do this, Master Brent. I can't let you whip my girl."

Brent's mouth fell open but he closed it again, quick, and growled, "Out of the way, Samuel."

"No, sir."

"Didn't you hear me? I said *get the hell out of my way*!" Brent's arm moved, and the whip described a lightning arc.

Samuel never flinched as the lash bit into his arm. A thin red line appeared but he didn't even look at it. "I'm askin' you nice not to do this, Master Brent. I don't want no trouble."

Brent's face was almost purple. "You will do as I say, or by God I will have you in shackles!"

"If that's to be, it's to be," Samuel said. "But you won't hurt my girl. No sir, not ever will you hurt my girl."

"Did you just threaten me? Did you just threaten your master?"

"Please, Master Brent. I'm askin' you, man to man. She's my child. What else can I do?"

Brent shook the whip at him. "You can listen to

your betters, is what you can do! I am through talking. For the last time, get out of my way."

From many of the shacks and out of the dark came other slaves, but they stayed well back. To interfere was to court a whipping, or worse. Randa heard a woman say, "Someone should fetch Master Justin."

"None of you move!" Brent roared. "This is between me and these upstarts. They must be taught a lesson."

"No, Master Brent," Samuel said.

"No, what? Hasn't it sunk through that wooly head of yours yet? You don't ever have a say. You don't ever tell me what to do. I tell you. And I'm telling you now, Samuel Worth, that you have stepped over the line. You have crossed a line no nigger should ever—"

"Don't call me that."

"What?"

"Don't use that word on me. I don't like that word. I ain't never liked it."

"Whites have been calling blacks that since before my granddaddy was born," Brent sneered.

"That don't make it right."

Brent shook his head in amazement. "The gall you have. Now you get to decide what is right and what is wrong? Is that how it goes? When did you become God Almighty? It would be comical if you weren't so stupid."

"There you go again."

Brent glowered and started to sidle to the right while wagging the whip at his side. "Enough talk. I have given you fair warning and you've refused to heed. What happens next is on your shoulders, not mine."

"Can't I just take my girl and go?"

Brent laughed, and the next moment his whip sizzled the air. It caught Samuel across the chest, opening his shirt and the skin underneath and drawing blood. Samuel simply stood there.

"What the hell is the matter with you? Didn't you feel that?"

"I felt it, all right," Samuel said sadly.

"Then let's see if you are so calm after I take out an eye." Brent grinned and drew back his arm to swing again, only to have his wrist seized.

Emala had taken all she could endure. She couldn't just stand there and watch her man be cut to ribbons. "Please, Master Brent. I'm beggin' you. Let me take them home and we can forget this ever happened."

Brent Sullivan reared as if to strike her, but instead he wrenched his arm free and stepped back. "How dare you lay a hand on me."

"I didn't mean to offend you, Master Brent."

Brent pointed at Randa. "Did you daughter mean no offense when she tried to cripple me?" He pointed at Samuel. "Did your husband mean no offense when he threatened me just now?" Brent swore bitterly. "Do you know what I think? I think your whole family are malcontents. I bet all of you have been talking behind our backs."

"Sir?" Emala said.

"Don't play the innocent. You've been listening to those whites up north who say slavery is evil and all you darkies should be set free. So now you put on airs and turn on those who provide the clothes on your backs and the food on your table." Brent turned to Samuel and raised his arm. "This whipping is just the start. I will see you hanged."

Emala couldn't help herself. She lunged and gripped hold of his arm a second time.

"Damn you!" Brent shoved her as hard as he could.

Tottering, Emala lost her balance and fell on her back in the dirt.

"Leave her be!" Samuel cried. He moved to help her to her feet. But as he bent, the whip cracked, and agony shot up and down his back.

Brent cackled and swung, laying the lash across Samuel's shoulders. Samuel made a grab for it, but Brent snapped the lash out of his reach and began to circle him. "Did those hurt? There's worse to come. A lot worse." He streaked the whip at Samuel's thigh and drew more blood.

Clenching his fists, Samuel stood over Emala, shielding her body with his in case Brent went for her.

"Cat got your turncoat tongue?"

"I've nothin' more to say, Master Brent. I've done told you all I care about is not havin' my family come to harm. I'll take whatever you dish out so long as they are spared."

"Who said they would be?" Suddenly whirling, Brent drove the whip out and down.

Randa was so afraid for her mother and father, she hadn't given any thought to herself. She was still on the ground, an easy target, and she cried out at the pain and the upwelling of blood.

"No!" Samuel started for Brent, but Emala clutched his leg. He tried to take a step, dragging her with him. "Let go of me, woman."

"No. I won't have you hanged."

Brent moved toward Randa as she frantically scrambled back, her elbows and heels churning. "This is your fault. All you had to do was give me what I wanted." He cracked the whip in front of her face, the lash nearly slicing her cheek. "I will carve you into bits and pieces."

"Noooooooo!" Out of the ring of onlookers charged Chickory. Fists flying, he yelled, "Get away from my sister! Stop hurtin' her!"

Uttering an inarticulate roar of pure rage, Brent backhanded Chickory across the face, knocking him to the earth. Chickory sought to get back up, but Brent slammed his boot down onto the boy's chest, pinning him. Brent's free hand disappeared under his jacket. "That was the last straw."

A dagger gleamed, and Randa screamed.

Samuel kicked loose of Emala. He reached Brent Sullivan just as Brent cocked his arm to stab Chickory. Samuel swung his big fist, intending to hit their mad-dog master on the jaw. But Brent heard him rush up and half-turned, directly into Samuel's fist. Samuel's walnut-sized knuckles connected with Brent's throat, not his jaw. Connected, and crushed it, as a sledge hammer would crush a melon.

Dropping the whip and dagger, Brent staggered. He placed his hands to his throat and tried to speak, but all that came out was a strangled whine, spittle, and blood. The whites of his eyes showed as he turned in a complete circle, then slowly sank down. A few twitches, a final gasp, and he was dead.

"Oh, Samuel," Emala said in the stunned silence that fell. "What have you done?"

Chapter Six

Nate King leaped to his feet and drew his pistols, but he didn't shoot. A wounded grizzly was fierce beyond belief.

Winona likewise jumped up and wedged her rifle to her shoulder. And she likewise didn't shoot. Should she miss a vital spot, the bear would be on them before she could reload. Armed with claws as long as her fingers and teeth that could crush bone, it would tear them to pieces. "Do we stand our ground or back away?"

Nate's every instinct was screaming at him to get out of there. If they could reach the horses before the bear reached them, they stood a good chance of escaping. Then again, over a short distance a bear was every bit as fast as a horse, or even faster.

"Husband?"

"We stand our ground." Nate had decided to rely on the tried and true. It might work. It might not. The only way to find out was to put the griz to the test. With that in mind, he raised his arms and hollered at the top of his lungs, "Get out of here, consarn you!"

The grizzly stopped at the river's edge. Dripping water, it regarded them with unnerving calm while ponderously swinging its massive head from side to side. Then it stopped swinging its head and growled.

"Go, you nuisance," Nate tried again.

The bear growled louder.

"We should slowly back away," Winona said.

Just then the sorrel whinnied in fright, drawing the grizzly's attention to the horses. Winona braced for a rush, ready to try to bring it down. They needed their horses. To be stranded on foot in the middle of the prairie would compound the dangers they faced. Worse, it would take them months to reach the Mississippi River.

Raising its nose to the wind, the grizzly sniffed.

Nate glanced at the frying pan. The scent of their food had drawn the bear in. Maybe he could appease it enough that it would leave them be. Bending, he snatched up the buffalo heart and held it out in front of him for the bear to see. "Is this what you're after, damn you?"

"Don't anger him," Winona said.

As if Nate would. He tossed the heart as close to the griz as he could without hitting it. "There. Eat it and go." For a few moments he thought the bear would ignore it.

Sniffing, the grizzly lowered its head. It nudged the heart with its nose a few times, opened its mouth, and the heart was gone.

"It will want more," Winona predicted. In her opinion, feeding the grizzly was a bad idea. Once its appetite was whetted, it might decide they or their horses should be part of its meal.

Nate picked up what was left of the buffalo tongue. He threw it and it landed with a *plop*.

The grizzly took a few steps and practically wolfed the tongue down. It stared at Nate as if expecting more.

"That's all you get."

The bear grunted.

"I warned you," Winona said. She fixed a bead on the bear's throat and thumbed back her rifle's hammer.

"Wait." Nate waved his arms and hopped up and down. "Leave us be! I've given you all I'm going to!"

The bear growled.

"I have a bad feeling, husband." Winona gauged the distance to her sorrel and realized that if the grizzly charged, it would be on them before she could mount. She edged closer to Nate. If they were to die, they would die together.

Nate yelled again, but the grizzly was not the least bit intimidated. Instead, it started toward them, moving slowly, its head low to the ground.

"It's going to attack." Winona touched her finger to the rear trigger to set the front trigger.

"Not if I can help it," Nate said. Loud noise hadn't worked. Feeding it hadn't done any good. He had one thing left to try. Turning, he grabbed the unlit end of a burning brand.

"That might make only make him madder."

"Let's find out." Nate held the brand in front of him and advanced toward the bear. He had to act before the flames went out.

The grizzly reared. It sniffed, and growled, and swung a huge paw at a smoky tendril.

"I will shove this down your throat!" Nate hollered, and sprang, thrusting at the bear's mouth and nose.

With a tremendous snort of displeasure, the grizzly dropped onto all fours and wheeled. Instead of running off, though, it looked back as if it had not made up its mind whether to go or press the issue.

Nate took a desperate gamble. Bounding forward, he jammed the fiery brand against the bear's hindquarters. Hair sizzled and burned, and the grizzly half-twisted as if to attack him. If it did, he would be clawed to ribbons before he got off a shot. Then Winona shouted and fired one of her pistols into the air, and the bear, with a roar that seemed to shake the cottonwoods, ran to the Platte and plunged in. Spray flew in its wake as it crossed. Presently, it clambered up the far side. Another moment and the vegetation swallowed its retreating bulk.

Nate waited to see if the bear would come back a second time. Heat on his hand prompted him to cast the brand to the ground.

"What do you think?" Winona asked.

"I think we should pack up, ride five or six miles, and make a new camp," Nate proposed. It was the only way to be sure.

"I agree." Winona had never told him, but she harbored a secret dread that a grizzly might one day be the death of him. Part of it had to do with his frequent encounters with the giant silver-tips back when they first became man and wife. Granted, the Rockies teemed with grizzlies then, before the tide of beaver trappers and the influx of settlers thinned their numbers. But still, it had seemed to her that Nate bumped into one every time she turned around, and she lived in daily fear that a grizzly would make her a widow.

"Damn bears." Nate did not like having to go to all the trouble to pack up and throw on their saddles and put out the fire. He added a few choice words he seldom used.

"Remember what we agreed about swearing," Winona said. The habit didn't make much sense to her. Among her people, a man who couldn't control his tongue was not held in high esteem. Whites, though, took delight in uttering streams of cuss words, usually with no more cause than venting their spleen. She witnessed many an outburst at the rendezous and trading posts and elsewhere. Fortunately, her husband never picked up the habit, which suited her just fine.

Nate kept an eye on the river, but the bear didn't reappear. In due course they were in the saddle and on the move. He let her go ahead of him so he could watch their back trail.

"That didn't turn out so badly," Winona cheerfully remarked. "Our luck, as you whites would say, still holds."

"The day isn't over yet."

"My goodness," Winona teased. "When did you become such a cynic?" She was proud she remembered that word. The whites had a wealth of language that she loved to mine.

"The day I realized we all die."

Winona shifted and stared. "What has gotten into you?"

"I don't know," Nate said. But he did. The incident with the buffalo earlier, the near disaster with the bear, had reminded him that life in the wilderness was a perpetual struggle. He tended to forget that fact now and then. And when he did, something came along to remind him.

Not that Nate regretted the decision he had made years ago, after the beaver trade died out, to stay in the mountains. He could have gone back east. A lot of trappers did. They were in it for the money, and when beaver fell out of fashion and the best of plews became next to worthless, they forsook the trapping trade for greener pastures.

But not Nate. For him, trapping was never about money. It was the freedom he enjoyed. The sense that he was his own man and could do as he pleased, when he pleased, and was never beholden to anyone.

Life wasn't like that in the States. Back east, people were ruled by law and society. They must conform, or else. Those who wouldn't or couldn't ended up as outcasts or behind bars.

Nate sometimes wondered what his life would have been like had he not answered his uncle's summons and come west. More than likely he would have gone on to be an accountant and spent his years chained to a desk, scribbling in a ledger.

Strange how life worked out, Nate reflected. Wanderlust brought him to the frontier; love kept him there. Love for Winona and the love of being his own man. He could never go back. He could never give up his freedom to be a cog in a machine.

"Husband?"

Nate came out of himself. He checked that the bear wasn't after them, then responded, "What is it?"

"There is death ahead."

Nate looked up. Through a gap in the trees he spied black shapes describing circles high in the air, and some not so high. There had to be two dozen or more. "Buzzards."

"What can have brought all of them?"

"We'll find out directly." The last time Nate saw so many was after a Shoshone buffalo hunt. He happened to gaze up while skinning and there had been scores of the aerial scavengers waiting for the Shoshones to leave so they could descend and feast. It was uncanny, that ability of theirs to wing in from all points of the compass when there were corpses and carrion to be had. Usually one buzzard would happen by and circle. Before long, there would be two or three. Within half an hour, the sky would be full of them. How they knew where to gather was a mystery. They didn't rely on sight, that much Nate knew, because once he saw several buzzards come winging over a mountain to join others feeding on a dead elk, and the new arrivals couldn't possibly have seen the elk from the other side of the mountain. He reasoned it had to be the same sort of thing that pigeons used to find their way to their roosts from hundreds of miles away, but what it was or how it worked was beyond him.

Winona drew rein and waited for him to come up next to her. "Do you smell what I smell?"

Nate nodded. The unmistakable stink of burning flesh. Not animal flesh, either. Human flesh had an odor all its own.

"I have a bad feeling about this."

Nate swung down, saying quietly, "Whites always say that bad things come in threes." First the buff, then the griz, now this. "Stay with the horses while I go have a look-see."

"Nothing doing." Winona swung a leg over her sorrel and slid down. "In case you have forgotten, I am your woman and you are my man. Where you go, I go."

"Even if I ask real nice?"

Winona snorted.

Crouching, Nate stealthily threaded through the thick undergrowth. He made no more noise than the breeze, with hardly a rustle of a leaf or stem.

Winona matched him, moving in perfect mimicry, stepping where he stepped.

The odor grew stronger.

Soon the trees thinned. Wary of being spotted, Nate slowed. They were near the prairie, and he saw the source of the smell. "Dear God."

Winona looked away, steeled herself, and looked back. "I never get used to it. No matter how many times, I never do."

Nate absently nodded. "It won't be the last time." Not with hostilities so widespread.

A stone's throw from the trees stood two wagons. Their teams were gone, and their canvas tops had been cut off. Belongings lay scattered everywhere, most smashed or hacked to bits, a few intact, everything from a butter churn to tools to clothes to a piano. But it wasn't the possessions that caused Nate's breath to catch in his throat. It was what was left of the people who owned them.

"I think one is still alive," Winona whispered.

So did Nate.

There were four, all told. Two men of middle years, a woman who had to be in her sixties, and a strapping young man who had not yet seen twenty. The first two had been lashed to wagon wheels and then things were done to them, things involving knives and tomahawks and body parts that were no longer part of their bodies.

The young man fared the worst. Staked out spread-eagle, he'd been stripped and then worked on with a knife. His eye sockets were empty, his nose was gone, and the ruin of his mouth exposed bared teeth where his lips had once been.

It was the old woman who was still alive. She, too, had been staked out and stripped. She had all her body parts. She just didn't have any skin.

Nate warily moved into the open. The tracks of unshod horses led off to the northeast. "Whoever did this is long gone."

"Dakotas, maybe," Winona said. "Or Pawnees."

The old woman weakly turned her head and her watery eyes blinked. She tried twice to speak, then croaked at Nate, "You're white, aren't you?"

Nate could barely stand to look at her. The human body without skin was hideous. "I am."

"They took my daughter and her kids. And Tom's wife. I could hear them scream as they were dragged off."

Nate said nothing.

"We were bound for Oregon country."

"Only the two wagons?" Nate was surprised. Normally, for mutual protection, whites traveled in trains of twenty or more.

"We thought we could make it on our own."

Nate waited for the inevitable.

The woman's watery eyes focused on his face. "I hurt, mister. I hurt awful bad. And I could be a long time dying."

"A long time," Nate agreed.

"Do me a favor, will you?"

Knowing full well what she wanted, Nate King nodded.

Chapter Seven

The Worth family ran.

They had no time to gather up their belongings, no time to pack a few clothes or grab some food. All they had were the clothes on their backs and the fear in their hearts.

Samuel Worth was scared, scared as he had never been scared in all his days. He'd killed a white man. For a black man, it meant dangling at the end of a rope. For a slave, it meant dangling at the end of the rope without even the formality of a sham trial. Once the whites caught him, he was as good as dead. There were no appeals from the summary court of racial bigotry.

Emala Worth, for once in her life, was at a loss for words. She was astounded by the turn of events. She was shocked by what Samuel had done. She kept telling herself that he didn't need to do it, that there had been another way to handle the situation. Now the whites would be after them, and she would lose her man. The thought made her quake.

Randa Worth still hurt from where Brent Sullivan hit her. She was glad the man was dead, glad he couldn't force himself on her or any other woman ever again. But she was afraid for her father, terribly afraid, and when he said they should run, she fled without complaint.

Chickory Worth was bubbling with excitement. His own pa, the kindest, gentlest man he knew, a man who never harmed a soul, who never spoke a harsh word about anyone, had killed a white man, and one of their masters, to boot. Chickory couldn't get over it.

Samuel led their flight. He knew the plantation as he knew the lines in his own palm, and he took them by rarely used trails and byways. They saw no one. The slaves had gone in from the fields and the Sullivans were at the great mansion. But it wouldn't be long before the alarm was sounded.

They had been running for half an hour when Emala puffed in pain, "I can't go another step. I am plumb wore out."

Samuel stopped. He had an ache in his side but hadn't said anything. They needed to put as much distance as they could behind them. He mentioned as much.

"I know," Emala gasped, bent over with her hands on her hips. "But I ain't used to this. This is the most I've run since I was Randa's age."

Randa was barely winded. She could run for miles without tiring. Nervously pacing, she said, "Thank you for what you did back there, Pa."

"Let's not talk about it ever again."

"Why not? You did what was right. He would have hurt me, or done the other thing."

"Hush, girl," Emala wheezed.

"I would die if he'd done that," Randa declared. "I'd slit my wrists or find some other way. No man does that to me, white or black. I don't care who they are."

"I said hush."

"What for? It's the truth, Ma. Why can't you face it? Just because you don't want to talk about it won't make it go away."

"Don't talk to your mother like that," Samuel said.

Chickory pointed to the east and exclaimed, "Look!"

Far in the distance fireflies moved. Only these were larger than normal fireflies, and their glow flickered when the wind gusted.

"Torches," Samuel guessed. "They're after us."

"I don't hear dogs yet," Chickory said.

"We keep runnin'."

Soon they came to the end of the trail. Ahead loomed dark woodland. They paused to catch their breath, and Emala said between gasps, "I don't want to go in there. I hear there's bears. And snakes."

"Would you rather I was hanged?"

"I'm only sayin'."

"We keep on."

"What if we take a wrong turn and end up in a swamp? I've heard awful things about swamps, too."

"We keep on," Samuel said, and did so. The others followed, Emala lagging. Samuel deeply regretted her having to exert herself so hard. She was in no shape for this, no shape at all.

The woods were an inky tangle that hindered and hampered them. They climbed over logs. They plunged through thickets. They waded through grass as high as their hips. Their clothes became dirty and sweaty and ripped in spots. They were cut and gouged and bruised. But they pressed on.

Samuel wouldn't let them rest. Not with his neck at stake. Randa and Chickory did fine but he had to constantly urge Emala on. She was doing her best but she was too stout.

Emala realized as much. She was sweating from every pore, as if she had been working all day in the blazing sun. Her body ached all over. When she breathed, her chest hurt. She let another fifteen minutes go by. Then she abruptly stopped and announced, "This is as far as I can go. You'll have to go on without me."

Samuel and the others stopped. "Don't be silly. I'm not leavin' you here or anywhere."

"I can't go another step, I tell you." Emala leaned against a willow. "I don't have it in me."

"We'll rest a short while."

"Go on, I say," Emala insisted. "I won't have you caught on account of me. I won't have you hanged."

Samuel turned to the children. "The two of you go on ahead. We'll catch up."

"We're in this together," Randa said. "I'm staying with you."

"So am I," Chickory said. He had never been alone in the woods at night. And his ma was right. There were bears.

Samuel moved to where he could look back the way they came. There was no sign of fireflies. But they were back there. The whites wouldn't give up. He was a marked man from that night on.

"Who would have thought it?" Emala said. "Us. Runners."

"If I had to do it over again, I'd just knock Master Brent down," Samuel said. "I didn't mean to kill him. As God is my witness, I didn't."

"What's done is done," Randa said.

"How can you be so cold?" Emala criticized.

"I'm not cold. I'm practical. Wishing Pa hadn't done it is pointless. He did, and now we must deal with it if we're to stay alive. The sooner you get that through your head, the better off we'll all be."

Samuel turned. "I told you not to talk to your mother like that."

"I can't help it. I'm mad. Ma acts as if we were in the wrong when it was Master Brent who should not have done what he did." Randa balled her small fists. "If you hadn't killed him, Pa, I would have."

Emala choked back a sob. "What's happened to us? What will become of this family?"

"We'll reach the Rockies and start a new life," Samuel vowed.

"But those mountains are so far," Emala said. "It'll take weeks to get there, won't it?"

"Months."

"How will we live? We have no money. We have no food. Dear Lord, Samuel, how will we live?"

Samuel took Emala in his arms. She pressed her face to his broad chest and quaked. "There, there. It will be all right. Have I ever let you down, woman?"

"No," was her muffled reply.

"We need to use our heads. That's all. We use our heads and we don't take chances unless we have to and we'll be all right."

Emala stepped back and looked up at him, her eyes glistening. "Oh, Samuel."

"What?"

"This family will never be all right again."

Chickory was watching behind them, and pointed. "The torches again. They're still after us."

Samuel scratched his chin. "I don't hear no dogs. How come they're not usin' hounds?"

"Could be they'll wait until the sun comes up," Chickory said.

"The dark don't make no difference to bloodhounds, boy," Samuel said. "They use their noses, not their eyes." He shook his head. "No, it could be Master Justin was off huntin' and took the hounds with him. He likes for them to flush bucks and whatnot."

"If that's the case, the Lord is watchin' over us," Emala said. She had a deep fear of dogs. When she was seven, her mother took her out of their shack late one night to see a runner brought in. The man was being carried on a long board. He couldn't walk. Not after the hounds got through with him. Emala still remembered the deep bites and the claw marks.

Randa said, "If the Lord was watchin' over us, we wouldn't be runnin' for our lives."

Emala straightened and jabbed a finger at her daughter. "Don't ever let me hear talk like that. That's blasphemin', is what that is, and I won't have no truck with it."

"Don't you two start in again," Samuel said. "Let's move on. We have a good lead but they'll come on fast."

"I wish we had torches so I could stop bumpin' into things," Randa said. "Next thing you know, one of us will step on a snake and be bit."

"You're a trial, girl," Emala said.

On they went. They took care to pace themselves. They didn't stop, but they did slow to a walk now and again. All four were exhausted. All four were torn and sweaty. Emala started to limp slightly but assured Samuel she was fine. Samuel came last, bringing up the rear.

Toward the middle of the night the woods ended

at the bank of a waterway. Elated, they sank to their knees and gratefully drank. Randa and Emala splashed water on themselves.

"Is this a river or a creek?" Chickory wondered, trying to peer across to the other side.

Emala looked about them. "Where are we, anyhow? We must have come twenty miles or better."

Samuel doubted it was that far. "I don't rightly know," he admitted. "But this is just what we need. They can't track us in water. And when they bring the hounds, the dogs will lose our scent." He stiffly rose, and gestured. "I'll go first. We'll hold hands and take it slow."

"How do we know it's safe?" Emala asked dubiously. "There could be sink holes. Or gators."

"Or snakes," Randa said.

"Splash and make noise and it will scare the critters off," Samuel advised. "Just don't let go of the person in front of you."

Emala shook her head. "I ain't goin' to do it."

"We have to."

"I ain't." Emala backed away from the water.

"We have to, I tell you, woman."

"And for the last time, no. Go on without me. I ain't steppin' foot in that river or whatever it is."

Chickory offered his hand. "You can walk with me, Ma. I'll keep an eye out for gators and snakes."

"It's not them, it's the sink holes." Emala wrung her hands in despair. "Or have you all forgot I can't swim?"

"There ain't nothin' to it," Randa said. "You just sort of lean back and kick your legs and you won't sink."

"I've tried that and I didn't float." Emala shook her head more vigorously. "No, sir. I refuse to drown. I'd rather be dog bit." Emala started to turn, but Samuel grabbed her by the arm.

"If there were any other way I would take it. But there's not, so you're comin' with us if I have to carry you."

Emala managed a grin. "That would take some doin'. I ain't exactly a feather."

"You ain't no cotton bale, neither, and I can lift them." Samuel pulled her toward the water, but she resisted. "Don't be foolish. We don't have time for this."

"Don't be callin' me foolish."

"I will if you are." And with that, Samuel scooped her up in is arms and waded into the water. "Here we go. Hang on tight."

Emala screamed and threw her arms around his neck.

"Chickory, you grab hold of the back of my britches," Samuel directed. "Randa, you take Chickory's other hand. If one of you flounders, the other give a holler."

"I hate this," Emala said into Samuel's neck.

"I ain't fond of it myself. But it's this or be caught, and I damn well don't want to be caught."

"What have I told you about your cussin'?"

"Yes, dear," Samuel said.

Dark water swirled about their legs, the level rising with each step. The farther they went from the bank, the stronger the current became. But it wasn't strong enough to pull them under, which eased one of Samuel's worries. "How are you doin' back there?"

"Just fine, Pa," Randa said.

"How far do we have to go?" Chickory asked.

Samuel peered into the night but couldn't see the other side. "Not far," he hoped. Something brushed against his leg, something clammy and slithery. He stopped, half expecting to feel the sharp sting of fangs, but whatever had brushed against him went on its underwater way.

Emala tightened her hold on his neck. "Is somethin' wrong?"

Samuel took another step and the water was suddenly up to his chest. "Careful," he warned his kids. "The bottom is slopin' out from under us." He gingerly probed with his left foot. The last thing he needed was to go under. Emala would panic, and could well drown them both.

"You're all tense. Why are you tense?"

Samuel was about to tell her she was mistaken when the water in front of them parted and up rose an alligator.

Chapter Eight

Samuel froze. He was struck with terror. Of all God's creatures, none was more merciless than a gator. He made out its long, wide snout and hideous eyes fixed intently on him. Emala had not seen it yet; her cheek was on his chest and her eyes were closed.

"Why did you stop, Pa?" Randa asked.

"We shouldn't just stand here," Chickory said nervously. "There's no tellin' what might come along."

Samuel wanted to tell them to hush, but his tongue was stuck to the bottom of his mouth.

"Samuel?" Emala stirred. "What's the matter? Why aren't you movin'?"

The alligator hadn't moved either. All it did was stare. Judging by the size of the snout, it must be huge. Samuel was content to stay where he was. He'd heard of gators ripping men open with a swipe of their razor teeth, or breaking men in half with a swing of their powerful tails.

"Samuel?"

Samuel found his voice. "All of you, be quiet."

Randa leaned to one side to see past him. She made out the outline of something in the water, something big, and it hit her what it was. "Oh my God! A gator!"

Emala glanced down.

Samuel felt her stiffen. "Not a sound!" he whispered, afraid she would scream and provoke the gator into attacking. He wasn't worried for himself, but for his wife and children. Death held no great fear for him, and hadn't ever since he realized long ago that the Reaper came for everyone in their time, and there was absolutely nothing a person could do about it except die with dignity.

Emala was petrified. The danger of drowning was bad enough. To be chewed apart by a gator was as grisly an end as she could conceive. She grew light-headed, and for a few moments she thought she might faint. But she willed herself to stay calm and looked the gator right in its reptilian eyes.

For an eternity neither side moved. Then, with a swirl and a splash, the gator turned and leisurely swam off, its tail lazily curling back and forth.

Samuel didn't waste a second. He plowed forward, eager to reach solid ground and safety.

Randa nearly lost her grip on the back of his britches. She stared anxiously after the alligator but it showed no interest in them. That didn't stop her from trembling at what could have happened.

Chickory was glancing right and left. Where there was one gator there were bound to be more, and he remembered the time a slave on a neighboring plantation had a leg ripped off. They were supposed to be rare in this part of the state, but rare was more than enough.

Joy coursed through Samuel as the water level fell from his waist to his knees. They were almost out. He waded faster and momentarily had his heart's desire granted—firm ground. He set Emala down and she leaned against him.

"That was too close."

Samuel agreed. But something told him it was just the first of many perils they would face on their long journey to the faraway Rockies. Clearing his throat, he said, "I was thinkin' to follow the creek north a mile or two so we could shake off the hounds, but that gator has convinced me to head overland unless one of you objects."

No one did.

"All right. Stay close together. We need to travel all night, I'm afraid, and rest during the day."

"We'll do what we have to, Pa," Randa said.

Their ordeal continued. Samuel had no notion of where they were, or where the nearest town or hamlet might be. He searched in vain for lights, but the night was as black as pitch.

Hours went by. Fatigue numbed them. Emala's feet were sore and her ankle continued to bother her. She'd twisted it when they were running. But she didn't demand they stop so she could rest.

Samuel's stomach took to growling so loudly, he almost punched his own belly. In exasperation he raised his eyes to the stars, and when he lowered his head, up ahead burned a light. Only one, but it was bright and clear, and where there was a light, there were people. "Look yonder."

"The Lord be praised!" Emala declared. "Maybe they'll give us food and shelter."

"We're runners," Samuel reminded her. "We can't ask for help. They'll guess, and turn us in."

"You don't know that."

Samuel grunted. Runaway slaves often had rewards on their heads. Not much in most instances, but greed came in all sizes. In his case, given he had killed a white man who was the son of a plantation owner, the reward was likely to be a lot, enough that every slave chaser in the state might come after them.

Some white men made their living doing nothing but hunting slaves. The hunters could cross any state lines, go anywhere, anytime, thanks to a law. Samuel wasn't familiar with all the particulars, but folks called it the Fugitive Slave Law, and what it meant was that the whites could do as they pleased hunting down blacks. But then, the whites had always done pretty much as they pleased when it came to anyone with a different skin color.

Samuel sometimes wondered what it would be like to be white. To live free and never be trod on. To be fair, he knew that not all whites were equal. Some were like the Sullivans, rich and powerful, with a fine mansion and plenty of land and all the fancy clothes and whatnot they could ever want. But other whites weren't much better off than blacks. They weren't slaves, but they lived hand to mouth, in shacks no better than his own had been, in clothes every bit as tattered as his, chained, as he was, to the yoke of human poverty.

Being poor was the worst a person could be. Being poor meant never enough food. Being poor meant never having good clothes. Being poor meant no future, whether you were black or white.

Samuel had given it some thought, and he'd decided there must be something wrong with people. Not just whites. With all people. That some could have so much and not care that others had so little smacked to him of more than greed. Emala and her Bible were well and good, but folks just didn't naturally love one another. For everyone, white or black, rich or poor, it was dog eat dog, and once at the top, the dogs with power lorded it over the dogs without. It was that simple.

Samuel hadn't mentioned his outlook to Emala. She would blister his ears with the Commandments and the Sermon on the Mount and say that all true goodness came from God and if a person wanted to be truly good all they had to do was reach out to Him. But if God was so good, Samuel couldn't help wondering, how was it He allowed some people to be slaves of other people?

Samuel gave his head a toss to clear it. He wasn't a deep thinker. Never had been and never would be. Too much thinking gave him a headache. It was better to take life as it came and not try to make sense of mysteries no man could puzzle out.

The light was nearer.

It turned out to be a lamp in the window of a farmhouse. Close by was a barn, and to one side of the barn a good-sized corral. In the corral were several horses.

"Surely not," Emala said when Samuel stared at the corral at some length.

"We could shake the men after us."

"Stealin' is stealin' and thou shalt not steal."

"Need is need," Samuel said, "and no one needs those horses more than we do."

"Please, no."

Samuel turned to his son. "I've got a job for you. It's important, and there's a risk. Think you can do it without gettin' caught?"

"Try me, Pa," Chickory said, practically swelling with pride. His father hardly ever asked him to do things beyond chores and such.

"Don't agree until you hear what it is." Samuel pointed at the farmhouse. "I need you to sneak over to that window and take a peek inside. See if anyone is movin' about. It's so late, everybody is bound to be asleep, but you never know."

"I can do that, Pa." Chickory went to run off but his father gripped his wrist.

"Not so fast. You can't let anyone see you. Not so much as a glimpse. Or they're liable to light a shuck for the sheriff and tell him they saw some runaways."

"I understand."

"Good." Samuel patted his son on the back. "Stay hid as much as you can. You never can tell when someone might look out an upstairs window and we wouldn't know they were there."

Chickory grinned. "I blend into the dark real well." He bent low as he cat-footed along the fence that bordered the pasture.

"There's nothin' we can do but wait," Samuel told his womenfolk, and wearily sat down.

Emala had her hands on her hips in the pose she took when she was angry. "Teachin' our boy to steal. My mama is rollin' over in her grave and I don't blame her."

"You're missin' the point of all this."

"Says you. But I'll humor you. What is the point I'm missin'? That we will stoop as low as need be?"

"Do I live or do I die, that is the point. If we're caught, I die. If you want a new husband just say so and I won't try so hard to stay alive."

"Don't be silly."

"Then don't you criticize when all I'm tryin' to do is go on breathin'. I'm no killer. Or thief. But now that I've killed, I have to steal to stay alive."

"Those horses ain't ours."

"Damn it, Emala. No, they're not ours, and it's

wrong to take them, but if takin' them keeps a noose off my neck, I will by God take them."

"I hate it when you talk like that."

"And I hate it when I'm doin' the best I can and all you do is pick me to pieces. If it will make you feel better, we won't keep them. Once we've gotten far enough away, we'll leave them with someone and ask that they be returned to their owner."

"We don't even know who the owner is."

Samuel sighed in vexation. "You are as good a woman as ever drew breath but you can be a trial."

Emala slowly eased down beside him and clasped his big hand in hers. "I don't mean to be. I'm scared, is all."

"And you think I'm not?"

"All we know is gone. All we had is lost."

"What did we have?" Samuel demanded. "We lived in a shack that wasn't ours on land that wasn't ours and worked crops that weren't ours for money that wouldn't be ours. We had nothin' is what we had." Samuel paused. "You know that ledger book the overseer is always writin' in? In the ledger book of life a slave is a zero because that's all a slave has."

"We had each other," Emala said defensively. "I had pots and pans and a rocking chair and my sewing needles."

"A whole heap of a lot," Samuel said sarcastically. "For all the years we've lived, we should have a lot more. We should have our own place, our own land. Somethin' we can leave for the kids when we're gone. Somethin' that shows we were here."

"Is that what freedom is for you? Is that why you're so all-fired set to go to the Rocky Mountains?"

"I'm set on it because there a man is really free. There's no law, Emala. No government. No one to tell us how to live. No one can buy and sell us as they please." Samuel gripped her other hand. "Don't you want to be free? Does the dream mean so little to you?"

"Your dream," Emala said. "But yes, I admit it would be nice. Awful nice. But I ask you, what do we do when we get there?"

"How do you mean?"

"I don't know much about the Rockies, but I do know livin' there won't be easy. What will we eat? What will do we for clothes? For that matter, where will we live? In a cave like a bunch of animals?"

"You're being ridiculous. I aim to build us a cabin. Before you say anything, no, I've never built one before, but that doesn't mean I can't. I'm right handy with my hands."

"What will you use for tools? And once we are in our cabin, what then? Do we live off the land? What about Indians? We hear stories all the time. Some ain't the least bit friendly."

"Why worry about all that when we haven't even crossed the Mississippi River yet?"

Emala fell silent.

Glad for the reprieve, Samuel watched the farmhouse. He didn't see his son anywhere.

Presently, Randa announced, "Here he comes."

Chickory came running bent over along the fence and crouched. "I looked inside, Pa."

"Were you seen?"

"No. There's a lady asleep on a settee. Other than her, I didn't see anyone else."

"On the settee?" Emala repeated. "Why would she sleep there when she must own a perfectly good bed?"

"She must have a reason," Samuel said.

"There's more," Chickory related. "She's got a gun."

"What?"

"A rifle is leanin' against the wall near the settee. I think she put it there so it's in easy reach."

"Maybe her man is away," Samuel speculated. "Maybe she has the rifle for protection."

"That ain't all she has."

"What else, son?"

"There's a dog."

Chapter Nine

A multitude of starry diamonds sparkled in the vault of sky.

Winona King lay on her back with her fingers laced behind her head, enthralled by the celestial spectacle. Even as a girl the night sky had fascinated her. Her grandmother had told her the stars were spirits, and Winona would stare up at the stars and wonder if she would become a star one day.

Now she knew better.

Nate said the stars were suns. He'd explained all that the whites knew of the universe. It made sense to her, but Winona couldn't get over how many there were, like the grains of sand on the shore of the ocean.

Nate also related the Bible account of a certain star that led the wise men to the babe of Bethlehem. That interested her because the Shoshones believed that once, long ago, a star led a great medicine man to the land of the spirit animals. At the time the Shoshones were in dire straits. Brutal people had come into their land, fierce men and women who lived in caves and slew many Shoshones. The medicine man went off to pray for guidance in how to deal with these invaders. The star appeared and he followed it.

The medicine man came to where the spirits of mountain lions, wolves, bobcats, coyotes and foxes lived. Their chief, a mountain lion spirit, told the medicine man that they would help the Shoshones if the Shoshones pledged from that moment on never to kill mountain lions, wolves, bobcats, coyotes or foxes.

The medicine man agreed and returned to the Shoshones to give them the good news. But many scoffed, saying he had never talked with the animal spirits. To prove he had, the medicine man touched a stone and it melted.

Later, the animal spirits caused the mountain in which the brutal people lived to melt as the rock had melted, and the invaders were wiped out.

Winona always liked to hear her grandmother tell that story and many others. When her own children were small, she told them as best she remembered them, and hoped that one day they in turn would pass on the tales to their children. It was how the old ways were remembered and honored. Among her people, anyway. With the whites it was different; they had books.

Of all her accomplishments in life, Winona was most proud of learning to read. Speaking a new tongue was one thing. It came easily to her. But the marks on paper had tested her mental powers as nothing ever had. She'd wrestled with them for many months, until suddenly, like a shaft of sunlight piercing the sky on a cloudy day, the light of understanding pierced her, and she could read.

In one of Nate's books Winona read about the stars, and about the moon, which did not die each month to be reborn, as her people believed, but swung around the world in what the whites called an orbit.

It never ceased to mystify Winona that for a people who knew so much, many whites were a lot like those brutal people who invaded Shoshone country long ago in that they saw everyone who was not white as different or inferior, to be used or killed as the whites saw fit. Nate had said that east of the Mississippi River, many tribes had been wiped out or forced onto reservations. He worried that one day his people might do the same to the tribes west of the Mississippi, but Winona laughed at the idea. There were too many Indians west of the Mississippi, powerful tribes like the Blackfeet and the Comanches and others.

Beside her now, Nate coughed and rolled over onto his back and let out a long sigh. He did as his wife was doing and placed his hand behind his head.

"Are you having trouble sleeping, husband?" Winona asked.

"More than usual," Nate allowed. He couldn't shake the old woman from his mind.

"We had a long day."

"A trying day."

Winona looked at him. "You must shut her out. You did what you had to."

"It's not just her. It's that bear. And the buffalo. We could have been killed." Nate bit his lower lip. "It could have been us the hostiles ambushed and skinned alive."

"It was not."

"But it *could* have been."

"So? We all die. The only question is when and how. Fretting over it is useless. What will be, will be."

"Where's the sense in it?"

"In what?"

"Dying? Why are we born only to die? Why are we put on this world if our only purpose is to have our lives snuffed out like so many candles?"

Winona sensed how deeply he was troubled and tried to soothe him by saying, "You ask questions only the Great Mystery can answer."

"You saw that old woman. You saw how much she suffered. She didn't deserve to die like that. No one deserves to die like that. But it happens all the time. Suffering. Death. It's almost enough to make a person think there's no rhyme or reason to anything. That this world is a living horror, and its maker must be a lunatic."

Shifting toward him, Winona placed her hand on his shoulder. "There are many more sunny days than cloudy ones."

"We weren't talking about the weather."

"You look at the bad in the world and you forget all the good. For every woman who dies like that old woman did, thousands die peacefully in their sleep. For all the horrors, there are many more joys. The joy of being in love. The joy of having a family. The joy of raising children and seeing them raise their children. The joy of simply being alive to enjoy all the other joys. Think of them and not the horror and you will be able to sleep."

Nate twisted toward her and smiled. "You always did have a knack for not letting your emotions get the better of you."

"That is how I was brought up," Winona reminded him. Among her people emotions were always held in check for the good of all. Village harmony came before all else.

"I still wish things were different, though. I wish no one ever had to endure what that old woman endured. I wish no one ever had to die."

Winona chose her next words with care. She had never heard him talk this way and it upset her. "You have a kind heart. It is one of the things I have always most loved about you. But life is not always kind. It can be cruel. That is why we must be like turtles."

"Turtles?" Nate repeated, and chuckled despite himself. "We should be as slow as molasses?"

"We must have a hard shell to protect our kind hearts so the cruelty in this world does not wear us down and break us."

"Keep our kindness locked away and only let it out when it's called for?" Nate said.

"No. We should always be kind. We only put on our hard shell when we need to."

"I never heard of a turtle taking its shell on and off."

Winona laughed. "At least you are smiling."

Nate drew her to him so her cheek rested on his shoulder. "Have I mentioned lately how much I love you?"

"Not since this morning." Winona rose onto an elbow and kissed him on the chin. "There is something I would say to you. Something you should be proud of."

"That you speak English better than me?"

"That you have always been a good protector. Not just a provider, a protector. You have made our home, our valley, as safe as you can, and you always keep the cruelty of the world from crushing us. I have never thanked you for that, and I would like to thank you now."

"A man does what he has to," Nate said.

"Not all men are as diligent. It takes someone with a big heart, a kind heart, to devote himself to his family above all else." Winona paused. "No wonder you are so bothered over the buffalo and the bear and that poor woman. You keep thinking about what could happen to those you care for, and it tears you apart inside."

Nate kissed her, and not on the chin. "You don't know the half of it. For a man, there's nothing worse than not being able to protect his loved ones when they need it most."

Samuel Worth was wet with sweat. Not from the heat, but from the raw fear that caused his heart to pound as he quietly opened the gate to the corral. Scarcely breathing, he glanced at the farmhouse. All was quiet. The dog inside hadn't barked. According to Chickory, it was asleep near the fireplace. Samuel prayed it stayed asleep.

The horses raised their heads and regarded him uncertainly.

"There, there," Samuel said softly. "I ain't here to hurt you. We just need to use some of you for a spell."

A roan nickered and stamped a front hoof.

Again Samuel glanced at the farmhouse. Nothing happened. Maybe the dog was used to the horses making noise. Turning, Samuel raised his arms over his head and windmilled them back and forth. It was the signal for the others to hurry across the pasture and join him.

Samuel moved toward the nearest horse. The animal let him come close and lay a hand on its neck. "Good horse," he said, patting it, and moved to the side to mount. Carefully gripping the mane, he swung up. He had only ever been on horses a few times in his life and wasn't much of a rider, but he could get by. He'd always wanted to own one, but horses were one of the many things a slave could dream about but hardly ever possess. "When I get to the mountains I will have my own," he vowed.

Chickory and Randa were helping Emala. She was limping worse than ever.

Samuel frowned. It was one thing after another. All he wanted was to get them safely away. All he ever wanted was to have them safe and happy and free. If asked, most every slave would say they would rather be free than a slave. But few ever shattered the invisible chains that held them to a life of servitude.

Breaking those chains was everything to Samuel. He'd harbored his secret passion for as long as he could remember. Even as a boy, he had hated being a slave. He hated having others tell him what to do. Hated being made to live where he did not want to live. Hated never having anything to call his own. Freedom would change that. A free man was master of his own life. A free man could make something of himself, and what he made was his and not anyone else's. Just being *free* was worth any sacrifice a man must make. Sometimes Samuel would say the word in his head and savor the sound as he would savor the sweet taste of honey. *Free. Free. Free.*

His family reached the gate. Emala leaned against the rails while Randa and Chickory moved toward horses.

"Go slow," Samuel cautioned. "We don't want to spook them."

Emala said, "This will never work."

"Pick a horse and climb on. Or do you need a hand up?"

"I need more than that." Emala slumped and put her hands to her face and said something.

"What was that?" Samuel asked.

Emala lowered her arms and stared aghast at the horses. "I've never been on a horse. I can't ride."

"There's nothin' to it," Samuel assured her. "You get on and hold on tight and the horse does the rest."

"There's more to it than that. And if I fall, I could break a bone. I'm heavier than all of you put together."

Samuel kneed his horse over to the roan and started to work it toward her. "I've got one for you. Grab hold of its mane. I'll get down and help."

"It's no use, I tell you," Emala said. "I can't do it."

Samuel did something he rarely did. He swore. "I never took you for a quitter, woman. You've always done me proud, but this is a side of you I can do without."

"Don't be mean."

"We're wasting time. See those lights off through the woods? Hounds or no hounds, they are still after us and unless you get on this horse and get on it right this minute, they will put a hemp noose around my neck and dangle me from a tree until I'm strangled. Is that what you want?"

"Now who is being mean?"

Samuel didn't realize they had raised their voices until suddenly Randa whispered for them to be quiet and pointed at the farmhouse. A face was at the lit window. The woman who had been sleeping was awake, and she was holding her rifle. She wasn't looking toward the corral but might spot them at any moment.

"Oh Lordy," Emala said.

Samuel clambered down. He ran to her and looped an arm around her waist. "I will put you on and you will ride and that will be the end of it." Hooking his other arm behind her legs, he lifted. Then, pivoting and swiveling his hips, he swung her up.

Squawking, Emala nearly went all the way over. She grabbed the mane and clung with all her might.

Samuel dashed to his horse. Randa and Chickory had mounted and were waiting for him to lead them. He was lifting his leg when Randa shouted a warning.

"The dog, Pa! The dog!"

A four-legged form hurtled out of the dark and teeth sheared into Samuel's calf. The pain was excruciating. Samuel cried out.

"Get them, Homer! Tear them to pieces!"

The woman was running from the farmhouse. Her dog, nearly as big as a calf and covered with bristly hair, bit Samuel again and shook his leg as if trying to rip it off.

The horses whinnied and milled in fright.

Flooded with agony, Samuel punched the dog's head, but the dog wouldn't let go. Emala screamed. In desperation Samuel lunged at the dog's neck, thinking to choke it into releasing him. But the dog leaped back and snapped at his fingers. He jerked them away just in time.

That was when the farm woman came flying into the corral with her rifle to her shoulder. "You leave my dog alone!"

Samuel wished the dog would leave *him* alone. He went to kick it.

"Don't!" the farm woman yelled, and pointed the muzzle at Samuel's forehead. "Or by God I will blow your brains out!"

Chapter Ten

The commotion, the growls and snarls of the dog, the yells and cries, agitated the horses. They nickered. They stamped. They turned this way and that. A few reared. A mare, frightened to the point of panic, chose the instant that the farm woman pointed her rifle at Samuel to bolt from the corral. The mare made straight for the open gate. And smack in the mare's path stood the farm woman, who was so intent on Samuel, she didn't realize her peril until it was upon her.

The mare slammed into the woman with such force she was sent flying against the rails. She hit hard, so hard that Samuel swore he heard bones crack, and then the woman was slumped on the ground, unconscious, and all the horses were racing out of the corral into the night.

Samuel swung onto his. He gave brief thought to turning back to see how hurt the woman was. But Emala was in front of him, flouncing and flopping fit to fall off, and concern for his wife eclipsed his concern for a stranger who just a few seconds ago was set to blow his brains out. "Stay together!" he shouted, and tried to bring his mount up next to Emala's. But he found that without a bridle, that took skill. Skill he didn't possess.

Emala was terrified. She gripped the mane so hard, her knuckles hurt, and clamped her legs fast to the animal's sides. She kept saying, "Whoa, horse! Whoa, horse!" To no avail.

Randa was behind her father. She sought to catch up but other horses were in the way. She didn't feel sorry for the farm woman. Nor did she regard stealing the horses as wrong. They must do what they had to in order to escape, and if that involved stealing, so be it.

Excitement coursed through Chickory. To have a horse under him was a treat. He had only ridden a few times, but it was enough to persuade him he would like a horse of his own one day. He experimented by tugging on the mane and found he could control the horse enough to keep the others in sight. He laughed with joy.

The horses were making for the forest.

Samuel slapped his legs to get his to go faster. The forest was a dangerous place. There were trees, briars and logs. It was no place to gallop through in the dark. But the panicked horses were not of a mind to slow down.

Emala saw the inky vegetation and squawked in alarm. This whole ordeal had become more than she could bear. Her peaceful world had been shattered, and she would give anything to have it back as it had been.

Another moment and the woods were all around them. Emala ducked to avoid a limb and felt it brush her hair. Another limb snatched at her sleeve. Yet another struck her leg, sending pain up her thigh. She was so scared she couldn't think of what to do. The horse wouldn't stop no matter how hard she pulled. She never had liked horses much, and she would never get on one again if she could help it.

Randa caught up to her father. She saw that he was having trouble and she flew past him to help her mother. The end of a branch lanced at her face, but she avoided it. A log appeared but her mount went over in a smooth jump. She grinned, pleased at how well she was doing.

Chickory was grinning, too. He was having no trouble keeping the others in sight. He figured his father would yell if they were to stop, and he was content to follow until then. Now and again he caught sight of his mother and almost laughed at how bad a rider she was. He wasn't worried she would fall off. It wasn't that hard to stay on.

Emala's terror grew until it filled her whole being. She glanced back, seeking Samuel, and screamed for his help. Randa was closing in on her, and Emala called to her, too. Leave it to her daughter to be of more help than Samuel. Small wonder that girl was her pride and joy.

Emala faced front. Too late, she saw another low limb. It caught her across the chest and lifted her clear off her horse. For a few moments she seemed to hang suspended in the air, and then she crashed to earth and horses were thundering past her on either side. It was a wonder she wasn't trampled.

"Emala!" Samuel bawled, and nearly tore the mane off his mount bringing his horse to a stop.

Randa halted first. Leaping down, she ran to her mother and threw herself to her knees. "Ma? Are you all right?"

Emala heard the words as if through a long tunnel. She was sure every bone in her body was broken and she was not about to move to find out. She wanted to cry, she was so upset, but she held the tears inside.

"Ma? Talk to me. Where do you hurt?"

"I hate horses."

"What?"

"The Lord help me, but if every last horse was to die, I wouldn't miss them. Can you see any bones stickin' through my skin?"

Randa checked. "No. But maybe you shouldn't move until Pa has a look at you."

"Don't worry. I won't. Where is he, anyhow?"

Samuel leaped down from his horse. "Is she hurt bad?" he asked Randa as he hunkered.

"I can't tell."

Emala swallowed and moved slightly, provoking new pain. "Are you happy now? You have gone and killed me. I'm busted to bits inside."

Samuel ran his hands down her arms and legs, then jiggled them. "I don't feel any broken parts. And you're not coughin' up blood. Maybe you're not as bad off as you think."

"It's my body. I ought to know when I am busted to bits. Leave me here to die. Take the children and go."

"You never stop sayin' silly things, do you?"

Emala reached up. Samuel, thinking she was groping for his hand, held his out. But Emala took Randa's hand, instead.

"Listen to me, girl. I see it all clearly now. Find yourself a good man and settle down somewhere. By good I mean a man who won't go around killin' white folks so you have to run for your life and end up lyin' in the dirt in the woods, busted to bits."

Samuel was growing indignant. "If you can talk that much, you can't be hurt that bad."

"Shows how much you know. Squished insides

don't keep a body from talkin'. I am just thankful I can impart a few last words to my daughter." Emala smiled at Randa.

"I want you to try to sit up."

"I want you to leave me be."

"I thought so," Samuel said. "You're mad at me so you're actin' like you do when I stay out late with the other men. Well, I won't have it, you hear? This is not the time for your shenanigans."

"Do you hear him, Randa? Find yourself a man who can tell the difference between squished and shenanigans and you will have a happy life."

"Oh, Ma."

Chickory brought his horse up next to them and leaned down. "What's goin' on? Why have we stopped? Why is Ma lyin' there restin' when we are runnin' for our lives?"

"That's what I'd like to know," Samuel said.

"It's males, I tell you," Emala said to Randa. "Why the good Lord made us from their ribs, I'll never know. I'm not one to second-guess the Almighty, but we might have been better off if we were made from chicken ribs."

"Just when I think you can't get any sillier," Samuel said in disgust, and rose. "On your feet, woman. You ain't hurt. You're just tryin' to make me feel bad."

Emala sat up. "I hope I succeeded. I am tired and sore and hurt and scared. Did you see what happened to that white woman? She might be dead, for all we know. Now it won't be just you they hang. It will be all of us."

Samuel hadn't thought of that. The idea chilled him.

"We'll be blamed for her dog," Chickory said. "I

saw it take a hoof to the head. Crushed like a melon, it was."

"Oh, Lord," Emala gasped. "Now we are dog killers, too?"

"We must keep movin'," Samuel said. "Everyone back on their horse. Emala, I'll give you a boost. Yours is stopped yonder."

"I have had my fill of ridin', thank you very much. You can eat that animal for all I care. I hear Indians do it, so they must be tasty." Emala stiffly rose. Samuel reached to help her, but she slapped his hand away. "I can do it myself." Pressing her palm to the small of her back, she winced. "I will be hurtin' for a month of Sundays."

"We could be dead, Ma, if we don't get a move on," Chickory said.

"All right. All right." Emala shuffled toward her horse. It was standing still and nipping at grass. "I am glad one of us is enjoyin' itself."

"Are you sure I can't give you a boost?"

"Samuel, we need to think things out. We have gone from bad to worse to worse than worse. If that white woman is dead, every white man in the state will be after us. Killin' a white man is one thing. Dependin' on the man, it doesn't always rile them. But kill one of their women and you would think it was Mary herself."

"Women are special to black men, too."

"Don't try to sweet talk me. I tried to keep you from goin' for Master Brent. I held on to your leg, and what did you do? You kicked me off. Now look at where we are."

Samuel stopped. "Would you rather he poked our daughter? You forget I was provoked."

"I ain't forgettin' nothin'. I'm just sayin'. Let's try

not to kill any more white folks if we can help it. If we keep on like we are, we'll leave a string of bodies from here to the Mississippi."

Soon they were underway. Samuel rode at the rear to watch for pursuit, and Randa slowed so she could ride alongside him.

"Don't take what Ma says too hard. She's upset. She doesn't really mean any of it."

"I know."

"But she does have a point. I could ride back and see if that white woman is still alive. Maybe then if they catch us they won't be as hard on us."

"We stick together. No matter what." Samuel was afraid that if they separated, they might not be able to get back together.

"How long before we stop? We've been on the move nearly all night."

"We'll ride until we drop," Samuel said. "It's life or death for us. We must stay ahead of them."

Randa glanced back and saw only darkness. "I want to thank you for protectin' me, Pa. That was somethin', you standin' up to Master Brent like that. Some would have let him do as he wanted."

"This would be a better world if everyone could just be nice."

Randa never loved her father more than at that moment. "What will life be like in this place we're goin'? The Rocky Mountains?"

Samuel shrugged. "I don't know a whole lot about them other than they are mountains and they are high. But we'll be free, and that's what counts." He paused. "You ever hear of Lewis and Clark?"

Randa had to think a bit. "Weren't those the two white men who went clear to the Pacific Ocean years ago? People still talk about them."

"That's them. You weren't alive then, but I was, and it was a big thing, what they did. They were as famous as famous could be. Just about every week there was a story in the newspaper, and your mother would read it to me."

Randa listened with interest. Her father never went on like this unless there was a point.

"It was grand, what they did. Goin' where no man had gone before. Seein' places far, far away. Them and those with them were the first. And one of those with them was a black man."

"No."

"Yes. His name was York. He was Mr. Clark's slave, and the papers would write about how he was a marvel to the Indians and a big help to Mr. Clark."

"Why a marvel?"

"Because the Indians never saw a black man before. The color of his skin, his hair, everything about him was new to them, and they would gather around and touch him as if he were the greatest thing they ever saw." Samuel laughed. "It tickled me when I heard that. But I liked what happened after even more."

"After?"

"The expedition was gone two years. When they got back, Lewis and Clark and most of the men took up their lives where they had left off. But some liked the Rocky Mountains so much, they went back. John Colter was one, and he became famous for findin'—what do folks call them? Geysers. Another who went back was York."

"He wanted to live in the wild?"

"He wanted to be free. The story I heard is that Clark wouldn't give York his freedom, so York ran off. He ended up livin' with the Crow Indians. For all

I know he might still be livin' with them. Livin' free." Samuel tiredly rubbed his eyes. "That's when I first got the notion of runnin' to the Rockies. If York can do it, so can we."

"Then you've been plannin' this a good long while?"

"Not so much plannin' as thinkin' how fine it would be. But I never really thought we would. I knew your ma would be dead set against the idea. Then this business with Master Brent happened, and here we are."

"Will we be happy in the Rockies, Pa?"

"I can't predict."

"I just don't want to get there and find out I hate it. It would make me so sad, I would cry."

"We'll make the best of what we find," Samuel told her. "The important thing is that we'll be free. If you have to cry, cry for joy. Cry for freedom, girl. Cry for freedom, because your life will never be the same."

"All we have to do is get there alive," Randa said.

"That's all."

"What if we don't? What if all of us are killed?"

"The important thing is the trying. And I'd rather die free than die as a slave. I'd rather hold my head high when I meet our Maker."

"Let's hope it doesn't come to that, Pa."

Chapter Eleven

St. Louis was a bustling beehive. The people never seemed to sit still for two seconds. Or so it seemed to Winona King, who was always amazed by the frenetic energy her husband's kind showed in their tireless bid to acquire that which they valued most: money.

St. Louis had been built on the money reaped from trade. Specifically, the beaver trade. During the heyday of the trappers, the city raked in over four million dollars. Once the fur trade faded, St. Louis switched its focus without breaking financial stride and became a leading port and major link between the civilized East and the untamed West.

Winona insisted on taking strolls around the city every chance they got. Nate didn't mind. He could use the exercise.

The city's riotous bedlam of seething humanity was divided into districts. Not so much by design as circumstance. Along the waterfront were the establishments that catered to the rivermen who plied the inner waterways and the seamen who brought in goods from far shores. They thronged the taverns and grogshops, drinking, gambling, and chasing skirts with zestful abandon.

The poor lived close to the waterfront, where shabby apartments and flea-ridden hovels could be had for a week's wages, if not more. Often, as they trudged about their daily drudgery, their eyes rose in envy to the fine homes and estates above the levee where the rich and generally well-to-do lived, some as lavish as palaces worthy of kings and potentates.

Sumptuous mansions, many three and four stories and made of limestone, boasted their owners' wealth with mahogany furniture and crystal chandeliers.

Nate had been to a few of the mansions and was duly dazzled. One was the home of William Clark, the same Clark who accompanied Lewis on their historic trek. Clark's main parlor was so huge, Nate jokingly swore he heard an echo when he talked.

St. Louis had cultural trappings to go with her commerce. Several newspapers competed for readers. Theaters put on popular plays. Haberdasheries catered to those with expensive tastes in apparel. Half a dozen establishments were devoted to dressing ladies' hair.

A steady stream of traffic plied the city's streets and alleys. Wagons of every type, carriages in gilded finery, riders on horses both fine and swayback, and a legion of pedestrians flowed ceaselessly from dawn until dusk.

At night the city's pulse quickened and the timbre of her character changed. The orderly beat of business gave way to the carnal pursuit of pleasure and vice. Glitter and greed shined bright.

At night St. Louis literally glowed. But for all her luster, those who were abroad after the sun went down did well to remember that the city had its dark side. Crime and violence were epidemic. It was said that St. Louis had more cutthroats and thieves than any city in the country, and Nate King didn't doubt it. On his first visit years ago he had nearly been robbed, so now, as he and Winona strolled about admiring the sights, he kept one hand on a pistol at all times.

They had arrived in St. Louis almost a week ago. Jake and Sam Hawken were both glad to see Nate again. Sam frowned when he saw Nate's rifle, and suggested it might be better for Nate to buy a new one than go to the expense of having it fixed. But Nate had owned the rifle a good many years and grown fond of it.

"If you can, let's fix her."

"It could take five or six days."

"We're in no hurry."

Winona didn't mind the wait, either. She got to see all the sights, and to shop. Now, wearing her best beaded doeskin dress, her arm linked with Nate's, she feasted her eyes on the sumptuous nighttime sights. As they came to a packed street lined with gambling dens and saloons, she remarked, "We are so different."

"You and me?" Nate said in mild puzzlement.

"Your people and mine. Compare all this," Winona said with a sweep of her hand at the chaos, "with a Shoshone village at night."

Nate chuckled. There was no comparison. Shoshone villages were quiet and peaceful, with only the occasional bark of a dog or laughter from one of the lodges to break the tranquility. Except when special celebrations were held, their nights were given to visiting and talking and smoking, to young lovers standing under blankets, to contemplation and council. A Shoshone village was serene. St. Louis was bedlam.

Suddenly a drunk appeared out of the throng, a bottle of rum in hand. Muttering to himself, he lurched toward them and bumped Nate's shoulder hard enough to make Nate break stride. "Watch where you're going, damn you," he slurred his complaint.

Nate balled a fist but Winona shook her head.

"Didn't you hear me?" the drunk demanded.

"Go away."

The man was big, almost as big as Nate, with dirty clothes and breath that reeked. His yellow teeth didn't help much in that regard. "I have half a mind to thrash you."

"You've got that right," Nate said.

"What?"

"You have half a mind."

The man grew red in the face. "I'll bust your skull for that," he growled, and raised the bottle.

In a twinkling, Nate had a flintlock up and out. But he didn't shoot. Reversing his grip, he brought the stock crashing down on the man's head. The drunk folded at the knees and dropped his bottle but gamely clawed for a knife at his hip. Nate struck him a second time, and in his anger he was the one who nearly busted the man's skull. As it was, they stepped around the prone form and moved on. A few glances were cast their way, but no one tried to stop them or stopped to help the rummy.

"We should go back to our room," Nate suggested. The incident had soured his mood. And he was treating her to a stay at one of the better hotels. The bed was soft enough to swim in, and the staff waited on them hand and foot.

"Don't be silly," Winona said. The spectacle of St. Louis's nightlife was a rare treat for her, and she would not be denied.

Nate sighed. Knowing her, she would want to walk around until nearly midnight. "Can we stop somewhere to eat, then?"

"Men and their stomachs."

"Excuse me?"

"I would love to eat. But at a place we have never been. How about there?" Winona pointed at a grogshop.

Nate imagined the seedy interior crammed with rowdy rivermen and food fit for goats, and shook his head. "We'll splurge and go somewhere nice."

"You are being very nice to me this trip," Winona remarked.

"I'm always nice to you. In case you haven't noticed, I happen to care for you more than I care, for, say, my horse."

"It is good you do, or I would go back and get that rum bottle and use it on you myself."

"For a Shoshone you're awful violent."

The next street was more to Nate's liking. Fewer people but classier places to eat. A sign boasting the finest food in all St. Louis caught his eye. Nate held the bronze-gilded door for Winona. Inside, the aroma of food mixed with that of pipe smoke. They only drew a few stares, and then only because of Winona. Indians were regular visitors to St. Louis, but few rivaled her in poise and beauty. Nate came close to hitting a man who openly ogled her. He held her chair out for her, commenting, "If that lecher looks at you again, I'll go over and introduce him to my tomahawk."

"And you claim Shoshones are violent? You will

do no such thing, husband. We must show we can be as civilized as anyone else."

A waiter in a red coat with silver buttons brought a fancy menu written in blue ink.

"Dear God. Look at these prices. This is civilization for you. They rob you blind and pretend they are doing you a service as they take your money."

"I can do without the grumpiness, thank you very much."

"I'm only saying."

"You also said we could splurge. That this whole trip we could treat ourselves. That since it was just you and me, we could have—what did you call it?—a second honeymoon?"

"Order whatever you want."

Winona laughed and reached across the table to clasp his hand. "You are adorable when you try so hard to please me."

"Don't ever tell Shakespeare you said that or I'll never hear the end of it," Nate responded.

"Where did that word come from, anyhow? Honeymoon? It has a nice sound but the moon is not made of honey."

"I don't know where it came from," Nate admitted. "And I don't know what the moon is made of, either. Although I read that some people think it's not much different than here, with animals and trees and rivers."

"There is a story my people tell. Back at the beginning of the world, the sun was too hot, and burned everything when it rose. So one morning Rabbit waited with his bow, and when the sun came up, he shot it with an arrow."

"A rabbit was using a bow?"

"Remember, husband, that my people believe

animals were much like us at one time. They could even talk."

"So what happened to the sun after Rabbit shot it?"

"Part of the sun became the sky and part became clouds and another part became the dark and its liver became the moon."

Nate chuckled. "The liver? What about its kidneys?"

"They became stars. The sun, too, became a star, but it was not as hot as before, so when it rose, it did not burn everything."

"That's some story."

"You should not poke fun. Whites have strange stories, too. Remember the one you told me about the horseman with no head?"

"By Washington Irving. One of my favorites. But he wrote that to scare people, not explain where the moon came from."

The waiter in the red coat whisked over to their table and gave a slight bow. "Have mister and madam chosen yet?"

"I don't suppose you have roast liver?" Nate asked.

"Behave," Winona said.

"Only the items on the menu, sir, and liver is not one of them. I take it you need more time?"

"Unless you have kidney pie."

"This isn't London, sir. Might I recommend the calf's head? It's quite popular. Our cook leaves the windpipe on, as some prefer it that way. He also scoops out the brains, mixes them with bread crumbs, and makes an excellent stuffing. If I do say so myself, we serve the best calf's head in all of St. Louis."

Winona said, "I would like to try that."

"Very well, madam. Do you prefer your brains plain or with butter and salt?"

"I am treating myself, so butter and salt."

"It comes with a side of succotash. And might I suggest ginger beer to wash your food down? It's a local favorite." The waiter turned to Nate. "Have you made up your mind yet, sir?"

"Chicken pot pie and apple brandy."

"A fine choice, sir. Our chickens are grown locally and plucked the day they are served. You won't find plumper birds anywhere." The waiter took their menus, bowed and smiled sweetly at Winona, nodded at Nate, and briskly departed.

"Isn't he marvelous?" Winona asked.

"He's your admirer, not mine."

"Why, Nathaniel King, are you jealous?"

"Let's just say that I wouldn't have been surprised if he started drooling. You made quite an impression."

"He probably does not get to meet many Shoshones."

"Especially Shoshones who fill out their dresses as nicely as you do."

"You *are* jealous?"

"Just hungry. You dragged me all over the city today. I now know St. Louis better than I know the back of my hand."

"Tomorrow we will be on our way. You are supposed to pick up your rifle in the morning."

Nate couldn't wait. Without his rifle he felt as if part of him was missing. In the mountains he never went anywhere without it. He never even stepped out their cabin door without the Hawken in the crook of his elbow. "Would you like to go to a play tonight?" Their second night there, he had taken her to see *The Tempest* and she enjoyed it immensely. They both regretted Shakespeare McNair wasn't along; he would have been in heaven.

"I would like to spend a quiet night," Winona said. "You can read one of the new books you bought."

A tingle of delight filled Nate. Reading was his favorite pastime. Or second favorite, depending on if Winona was feeling frisky. One of his new books was by an author he highly admired, James Fenimore Cooper. It was entitled *The Pathfinder or The Inland Sea,* and continued the adventures of the Leatherstocking Natty Bumppo, or Hawkeye as the hero was more commonly known. Which surprised Nate considerably, given that in Cooper's previous book about Bumpo, *The Prairie,* Natty Bumppo died.

Their food came, and Nate had to admit the chicken was tasty. Winona loved her calf's head and shared the breaded brains with him.

That night Nate lay cozy and warm in a soft downy bed and read his cherished Cooper until his eyelids were too heavy to stay open. They awoke at six, had breakfast next door, and were at the Hawken brothers' shop at the appointed hour of nine A.M.

Nate's rifle was as good as new. As always, the Hawkens had done superb work.

Samuel watched Nate fingering it and restlessly shifted his weight from one foot to the other.

"Relax," Nate said. "I couldn't be more pleased."

"It's not that," Samuel said.

"Then what?"

"I have a question to ask and I'm not sure how to go about it, so I might as well come right out with it." Samuel took a deep breath. "How do you feel about blacks?"

Chapter Twelve

"What kind of question is that?"

Samuel Hawken crooked a finger for Nate and Winona to follow him to the back of the shop. Once they were out of earshot of the other customers, he said quietly, "You'll understand better in a moment, but it's one I need to ask. Some people don't like blacks. Usually the same people who don't think much of Indians."

"Bigots," Nate said. Putting his arm around Winona, he declared with a grin, "As you can see, the color of a person's skin doesn't matter much to me."

"Much?" Winona said.

"I had to ask," Samuel insisted. Again he crooked a finger and led them out the rear door.

The morning sun splashed over them. Four people sitting on the ground rose to their feet. Four blacks. A family, Nate guessed. The man was big and broad, the woman heavyset. Their daughter was quite lovely, their son sinew and bone. All four wore clothes that looked fit to come apart at the seams. All four were plainly worn and tired. The mother nervously smiled. The father offered his calloused hand.

"Nate and Winona King," Samuel introduced them, "I'd like for you to meet the Evans family.

This is Lester, his wife Rassa, their daughter Sarah, and their son Martin."

"Pleased to meet you," Nate said. He noticed how Lester glanced down at his hand as if surprised by the strength of Nate's grip.

"Yes, pleased," Winona echoed.

Rassa Evans said anxiously, "We're pleased to make your acquaintance, Mrs. King. We hope you are able to help us."

Nate arched an eyebrow at Samuel Hawken.

"Here's the situation. Lester, here, has heard that our shop is a gathering place for every frontiersman who passes through St. Louis. Even those who don't need guns know they can get the latest news about anything and everything having to do with the frontier."

Nate grunted. It was true. The Hawken shop was better than a newspaper when it came to all the latest information.

"They figured, and rightly so, that here they could find the person they need to help them with the next stage of their journey." Samuel paused. "You see, they're bound for the Rockies."

Nate looked at them again and was troubled by what he saw.

"That's right, sir," Lester Evans said. "We need us a guide to get us there, and Mr. Hawken was kind enough to say he could find us one."

"We're hopin' you will take us," Rassa said quickly, "if that's where you're bound. And the sooner, the better."

"Real soon," their daughter stressed, earning sharp glances from both her father and mother.

"Why do you want to go to the Rockies?" Nate came right out and asked.

"To live," Lester Evans said. "I plan to build us a cabin. We're goin' to live off the land like the Indians do."

Nate hid his surprise. Tactfully, he brought up, "It's not like living back east. You can't plant seeds and expect the land to give up her bounty. You have to wrestle with life day in and day out. It's hard work just to stay alive."

"But beggin' your pardon, sir," Lester said. "You've done it, and others like you. Me and mine can, too, if we put our hearts and minds to it."

Nate was skeptical. Their accents hinted they came from the Deep South, where the climate was warm and the land fertile. Where hostiles were few and the only wild beasts were timid black bears and rare mountain lions. "I can't help wondering if you know what you're in for."

"We're goin' whether we find us a guide or not," Lester said. "But we would be grateful if you would take us."

Rassa added, "We won't be no bother, Mr. King. No bother at all."

"It's not that," Nate said.

Winona wondered why her husband was so dead set against guiding them. She was fascinated by the four. They were the first black family she had ever met, and she was eager to get to know them. "I want to help them, husband," she interjected.

Nate gazed to the west, stalling to gather his thoughts. His every instinct was to say no. He didn't want their lives on his conscience. "You're safer staying east of the Mississippi."

"Beggin' your pardon, again, sir, but shouldn't that be for us to decide?" Lester responded.

"I think it should," Winona agreed.

Nate smiled and took her hand, saying to Lester and Rassa, "Will you excuse us while we talk it over?" He moved off under a maple and turned his back so the family couldn't hear what he was saying or read his lips. "What do you think you're doing?"

"I was about to ask you the same thing," Winona said. "They need our help. Why do you hesitate?"

"Look at them," Nate said. "Take a real good look. Do you really think they have any idea what they are getting themselves into? Do you want their deaths on our heads?"

"They appear to be nice people."

"That's not the point."

"That is exactly the point. Our friends the Wards knew nothing about the mountains when they came west, and look at them now. We helped them settle and they are doing fine."

"This is different," Nate said.

"Why? Because they are black and the Wards are white?"

"I'm shocked you would say such a thing to me."

"Then how is this different? Explain it to me so I will understand."

Nate was going to tell her there might be more involved but he could tell it was pointless. She had her mind made up, and trying to change it was akin to beating his head against a maple tree.

"Look at it this way," Winona said. "You are the one who believes the hand of Providence is in all things."

"So?"

"So they need a guide to the mountains. We are about to head back. Providence brought us together so we can help them."

Nate smothered a flash of annoyance. She had a

knack for using his own words against him. "There might be more to this than you think."

"How so? And even if there is, they need our help. That is what this boils down to. Nothing else matters."

Sighing, Nate shrugged. "Fine. You've made up our minds. But, remember, this was your idea." Wheeling, he strode over to the family. They were waiting expectantly, Rassa wringing her hands.

"Will you guide us, sir?" Lester asked.

"We leave in half an hour. Meet us out front of the gun shop. We'll take you with us."

All four beamed. Lester gripped Nate's hand and pumped it. Tears trickled down Rassa's cheeks and she dabbed at an eye with her sleeve. Their son was so excited, he yipped and spun in a circle.

"You don't know what this means to us, sir," Lester said.

"I think I do." Nate pried his fingers loose. "And you can stop calling me sir. I answer to my name."

"Yes, sir." Lester started to hurry off. "In half an hour, out front. We'll be there. I promise."

Winona came up behind Nate and hooked his elbow with hers. "Look at how happy you made them. You should feel good inside."

The truth was, Nate felt as if storm clouds were on the horizon and they were about to ride right into them.

As soon as they were out of sight of the Kings, Samuel Worth wrapped his arms around Emala and gave her a squeeze in pure delight. "We've done it! We are as good as in the mountains!"

"We shouldn't have lied."

"The Hawken brothers told me Nate King is one

of the best there is at findin' his way around and livin' off the land."

"It was wrong."

"He has a family too. A boy and a girl. Sam Hawken says the boy is married and the girl is about Chickory's age, maybe a little older."

"Thou shalt not lie," Emala said crossly. "Lordy, we have been breakin' commandments right and left."

Samuel lost some of his exuberance. "What are you on about now, woman? Must you always carp?"

"We lied. We didn't tell them our real names."

"What good would that do?" Samuel snapped. "By now word has spread. I doubt there's a lawman between Georgia and here who ain't on the lookout for us. And Master Frederick is bound to have posted a bounty, which means the bounty men are after us, too."

"All the more reason for us to tell the Kings," Emala said. "They need some idea of what could happen."

"Once we reach the Rockies it won't matter. The law can't touch us there. And the bounty men ain't about to go that far."

Emala would not let it drop. "They will if the bounty is big enough."

Randa said, "What puzzles me, Pa, is how we've come so far without once seein' sign of a slave hunter on our trail."

"We're too sneaky and smart," Chickory boasted.

Samuel wasn't so sure about the smart part, but they had been sneaky. They'd only traveled at night, for one thing. They fought shy of towns and cities, for another. Always sticking to back roads took longer, but they hardly ever saw another living soul. It helped that most country folk went to bed early.

They still had the horses they'd stolen. Traveling on foot would add months to their journey, so Samuel elected to hold on to them. He'd promised Emala that he would return the animals somehow once they no longer needed them. He didn't mention that once they reached the mountains, they would need the horses more than ever.

As for food, Samuel wasn't proud of having to raid so many farms late at night. He wasn't proud of the eggs they took. He wasn't proud of the occasional chicken or pig they helped themselves to. They didn't eat regularly, but they ate enough to keep their strength up, and that was the important thing.

Now here they were, in St. Louis. Samuel could hardly believe it. His dream of being free was on the verge of coming true. All they had to do was cross the Mississippi and the prairie and they could begin their new life. Suddenly he became aware that Emala was talking to him.

"—listenin' to me? I won't be ignored, you hear."

"Sorry," Samuel said.

"I still think we should tell the Kings the truth."

"When?"

"When we meet them out front of this here gun place. It would set my mind at ease."

"But what if it changes theirs? What if they don't want to take us once they find out we are runaways?" Samuel shook his head. "No. We keep quiet. You can tell them once we are safe in the mountains but not before."

"So it's come to this, has it?" Emala said sadly.

"Don't start with me. I am doin' the best I know

how to keep us from bein' caught. Or do you want us taken in chains back to Georgia and have me swingin' from the end of a rope?"

"You bring that up a lot."

"Only because you keep forgettin' what's at stake," Samuel said harshly. "Pretty near once a day I have to remind you why we are on the run."

Emala averted her face. She was on the verge of tears. A common condition these days. But she would be strong for the children's sake, if nothing else. "It just bothers me to go against how I was brought up. My ma raised me to always do as the Bible says, and I've tried to do the same with us."

"Your Bible will be the death of me."

Shock caused Emala to take a step back. "Samuel Worth! Don't ever let me hear you say a terrible thing like that ever again. All the good in this world comes from the Bible. It's the Word of God and I will not have it belittled, you hear me? Why, that's the same as belittlin' the Almighty Himself."

Samuel bit off a sharp reply. It wasn't that he didn't believe, or that he didn't hold Scripture in high regard. But there were times, and this was one if ever there was one, when living as the Bible said to live could get a man killed. And when it came down to it, Samuel was too fond of living to let himself be hauled off and strung up.

"Nothin' to say?"

"If you're so all-fired set on gettin' rid of me, then you go ahead and tell the Kings who we are. Tell them I killed a man. Tell them we're runaway slaves. Tell them bounty men are likely after us. And when they say they don't want to take us to the mountains, it'll be your fault. When the bounty men catch us and take us back, it will be your fault.

And when I'm swayin' from a noose, that will be your fault, too."

The tears Emala had been holding back filled her eyes.

Chickory said, "I'm tired of you two fightin' all the time. Why can't you get along like you used to?"

"Things change, boy," Samuel said.

"Stay out of this," Emala snapped.

"I don't want Pa dead, Ma," Randa said.

"You too, daughter?"

"Me too. You always say how I can be pigheaded, but you can be just as pigheaded as me." Randa put a hand on her mother's arm. "Please, Ma," she begged. "Please."

Wiping her eyes, Emala coughed to clear her throat and said softly, "Very well. Not a word to Nate and Winona King until we reach the mountains. And God help us if they lose their lives because of us."

Chapter Thirteen

To say Nate King was surprised was an understatement. Astounded was more like it. He stared at the four in their threadbare clothes astride their bareback mounts and asked in disbelief, "Is this it?"

"Beggin' your pardon, sir?" Samuel said.

"Where are your supplies? Your guns?" Nate bobbed his chin at their horses. "Where are your saddles? Your bridles?"

Samuel had been expecting the questions and had his answers ready. "We plan to live off the land as we go. It's summer so it shouldn't be hard. As for guns, I've never owned one my whole life long and wouldn't hardly hit much if I had one."

When he didn't go on, Nate prompted, "And what about your saddles and bridles? Don't tell me you intend to ride all the way to the Rockies like that." He wondered if they had any idea how far it was. Or the perils that might crop up.

Samuel hesitated, and Emala came to his rescue. "We don't own any of those things, Mr. King. We're poor folks. All we have are the clothes on our backs and love in our hearts. That, and our Maker to watch over us."

Nate had never seen the likes of them. Even he, as

adept as he was at surviving in the wild, would not think to cross the plains unarmed and bareback. It was tantamount to inviting calamity. "This just won't do."

"Sir?"

"You need supplies. You need flour and other food to tide you over when game is scarce. You need rifles to keep hostiles and beasts at bay. You need saddles so you don't chafe your backsides, and you need bridles so you can handle your horses better."

Fear spiked Samuel, fear that the mountain man wouldn't take them. "But you don't have no flour or whatnot. And with all the guns you're totin', none of those hostiles or critters will come anywhere near us." He patted his horse. "We don't mind bareback. We truly don't. As for bridles, we've gotten by this long without them."

Nate was about to give voice to a whole host of objections. But just then Winona caught his eye and reined to one side. "Excuse me," he said to the Evans family. Gigging his bay over next to her mare, he said so only she would hear, "I've heard of hare-brained, but this beats all."

"They are poor, the mother said," Winona reminded him. She had taken an instinctive liking to Rassa; the woman had a kindly face.

"They'll be dead if they try to cross the prairie like that."

"Not with us to watch over them. We will hunt enough to fill their bellies as well as ours, and we will share our flour and coffee." Winona held up a hand when Nate went to speak. "I know it puts us to extra bother, but I am willing if you are."

"And once we get them to the mountains, what

then?" Nate said. "How long will they last without guns and food?"

"What is the white saying? Oh, yes. We will cross that bridge when we come to it. For now, we will stop at the store down the street and buy some rope. We do not have enough money to buy saddles for all of them but we can rig the other."

Nate knew what she had in mind. "Just remember. If things go wrong, I was dead set against this." He reined around. "I guess we're still taking you," he announced. "But first we have to visit the general store."

No one asked why or what he was up to when Nate came out with a coil of rope, drew his bowie, and commenced cutting. Holding a piece the proper length, he stepped up to the father's mount.

"What's that?" Samuel asked.

"A rope bridle. Indians use them all the time." Nate fashioned a lark's-head knot and slipped it over the horse's lower jaw. When it was snug, he handed the ends to Lester Evans. Then he went from horse to horse, cutting rope and doing the same. He did Rassa's mount last.

"We thank you, sir, for your kindness. These are the first horses we've ever—" she seemed to catch herself, "—owned, and there's a lot we have to learn yet."

Nate noticed how she sat on her horse. "How well can you ride, if you don't mind my asking?"

"I flop around somethin' awful," Emala said with a warm smile. "I just can't seem to help myself."

Nate glanced at Winona, then climbed back on his bay. He didn't say a word as he led them out of the city. Long ago he had learned to rely on his gut, and his gut feeling was that they were making a terrible mistake. But Winona wanted to do it, and he'd never refused her, not in all the years they were together.

St. Louis had swelled to over sixteen thousand souls and was still growing, and those souls needed more and more land. It took a while to put the city behind them.

The road was well traveled. It would eventually bring them to St. Joseph, the stepping-off point for emigrants bound for Oregon Country.

At noon they passed a long line of prairie schooners. Later, they came on over twenty heavily laden freight wagons bound for distant Santa Fe. A steady stream of locals in buckboards and buggies, riders, and people on foot, added to the mix.

The lush green of the rolling Missouri countryside was pleasing to the eye. Thick forests of oak and hickory predominated, but there were also heavy growths of cypress, elm, and ash. Goldenrod, dogwood and milkweed were abundant. Splashes of flowers added drops of color.

That night they camped in a clearing beside the road, and Nate went off into the woods and shot a rabbit. Winona butchered it, cut the meat into pieces, and impaled the pieces on sticks. She gave one to each of the Evans family. When she held hers over the fire, they did the same.

Nate had put coffee on to brew. Filling his tin cup, he held it out to Lester. "Have some."

The aroma made Samuel's mouth water. It had been weeks since he had tasted coffee, but he shook his head and politely said, "I couldn't, sir. Not until after you do."

Winona noticed how the children tore into their pieces of rabbit like starving wolves. She had assumed they were naturally thin, but now she wondered. She almost asked them when they had eaten last, but she decided that might embarrass them. "Tomorrow night you should shoot a deer," she said to Nate. "I have been hungry for venison."

Emala, chewing happily, remarked, "This is nice, missus. We have been on the go so long, I almost forgot how nice life can be."

"You have had rough times?"

"Oh my. You don't know the half of it," Emala began, but stopped herself from going on.

Samuel had been wanting to ask something all day, and now he did. "Tell me, Mr. King. You ever meet the Crow Indians?"

"I know some of them well," Nate said. They weren't quite as friendly toward whites as the Shoshones but they didn't kill whites on sight, like the Blackfeet.

In his excitement, Samuel sat forward. "Is it true there's a black man livin' with them?"

"It's true," Nate confirmed.

"And this black man, was he once with Lewis and Clark? Is his name York?"

Nate nodded. "He's been with them a long time, and they think highly of him. So highly, they've adopted him into their tribe. Last I heard, he had four wives."

Emala gasped.

"Four?" Samuel said. "What on earth would he want with that many women?"

"A warrior can have as many wives as he can support," Nate explained, and when they still looked perplexed, he went on. "Among some tribes, there are more women than men. Take the Crows. A while back they were hit by smallpox. That, and war with other tribes, has cut their numbers to where the women outnumber the men about two to one."

"My word," Emala said, and gave her husband a pointed look. "One thing is for sure. We won't be takin' up Indian ways. Not while I'm breathin'."

"Fine by me," Samuel said. One woman was more than enough, in his opinion. There was only so much nagging a man could take.

Samuel Hawken was closing the shop for the night. He had just locked the door and turned when five men bristling with weapons and leading their horses by the reins came down the street. The man in front held the leash to three bloodhounds, all of which had their long noses to the ground and were sniffing loudly.

The man was short and thick-shouldered and wore some of the dirtiest homespun clothes ever worn by a human being. He had no hat and no hair to speak of, and the sun had burned his bald pate the color of burnished copper. His dark eyes glittered as he gave the leash a sharp tug and the bloodhounds came to a stop. "Sit," the man said, and the hounds sat. He glanced at the sign above the door, and then at Samuel. "How do, mister?" His Southern accent was thick enough to cut with a butter knife.

"Fine dogs you've got there," Samuel said.

"That they are," the man said, smiling. "Paid top dollar for them, and you won't find better trackers in all of Georgia, or anywhere else besides."

"Georgia, eh? You're a long way from home."

"That we are," the man agreed amiably. "We're after four runaway slaves."

"You don't say," Samuel said.

"I do." The man switched the leash from his right

hand to his left and held out his right. "They call me Catfish on account of I like to eat it more than I like to eat anything."

"If you're in need of a firearm, I'm afraid you must come back tomorrow. It's been a long day and I'm eager for my supper."

Catfish chuckled. "We have enough guns to outfit a regiment. No, what we're after are those four slaves. I don't suppose you've seen them?"

"I haven't had a black man in my shop since Moses Harris paid me a visit a month ago," Samuel said.

"Who?"

"A mountain man. He was a trapper for a spell. Now he mainly works as a guide."

"Oh. A free darkie, is he? They don't interest us none." Catfish regarded his dogs. "What does interest me is that the slaves I'm after came right past your shop. Maybe you saw them, but it's slipped your mind. A family of four. The pa is as big as a black bear and the ma could be mistook for a hog."

"Escaped slaves, you say?"

"They killed a white man and have been on the run ever since. Their own master, it was. His pa is offerin' a five thousand-dollar bounty for their return, which me and my friends aim to collect."

Samuel whistled. "That's a lot of money."

"You bet it is. Which is why we're not the only bounty men after them. And why I was hopin' you could tell us which direction they took after they left."

"I'm sorry. I can't be of any help to you gentlemen." Samuel touched his hat and departed.

One of the bloodhounds growled.

"Hush, Big Red," Catfish commanded, and the

dog fell silent. Catfish watched until the gunsmith turned a corner, then faced his companions. "He was lyin', boys. Lyin' through his teeth."

"He was?" said the youngest of the riders, a gangly youth with a straw thatch and buck teeth.

"As sure as I'm standin' here, Joe Earl. I could see it in his eyes."

"Then shouldn't we go after him and make him tell us what we want to know?" Joe Earl asked.

"This ain't Georgia, boy," Catfish reminded him. "The Supreme Court gave us the right to hunt down fugitive slaves. It didn't give us the right to beat on white folks who take us for fools."

The biggest of them, a muscular hulk with a bushy black beard so long that it covered his broad chest, said with a gruff rumble, "Folks like that make me mad. I'd as soon kick their teeth in."

"Save that violent streak of yours for when we catch up to the darkies, Trumbo," Catfish said. "But don't overdo it. Frederick Sullivan is payin' more for them alive. Dead, we only get two thousand."

A third man, his broad nose and pockmarked face lending him the likeness of a swarthy toad, chuckled and said, "We know why old man Frederick wants them alive, don't we? So he can punish them himself. Especially the one that done murdered his son."

"You can't blame him, Pickett," Catfish said. "I sure wouldn't want to be that wooly head when Frederick gets his hands on him."

The last member of their party swore. He wore buckskins, and his rifle was a fine Kentucky. "Are we goin' to sit here jawin' all damn day or get after them? I'd like to make it home before the leaves change color."

"Oh, hell, Wesley," Catfish said. "It won't take us

but another month, if that. We're close. Awful close. And since we know where they're bound, they ain't likely to give us the slip."

"We do?" young Joe Earl said.

"Haven't you wondered, boy? Haven't you asked yourself why these four keep headin' west when most every slave we chase heads north? North is Yankee country. North is bleedin' hearts who reckon they can change the world. North is safe for runaway slaves. But these four keep headin' west."

"Maybe they can't tell direction," Pickett said, and everyone laughed.

"There's no maybe about it," Trumbo declared. "Darkies are as dumb as tree stumps."

"Not these four," Catfish said. "They can tell direction just fine. They're headin' for the frontier, and beyond, unless I miss my guess."

"Beyond?" Joe Earl said. "But that's Injun country. And I ain't of any mind to tangle with Injuns."

"Calm yourself, boy," Catfish said. "It won't come to that. Likely as not they're headed for St. Joe. It's the last town before the prairie. And it's more than three hundred miles from here to there. Plenty of time for us to catch up to them." Catfish grinned and patted his favorite hound. "Mark my words. Before the end of the week, those blacks will be in chains."

Chapter Fourteen

An island of brown and gray in an ocean of green, the hamlet consisted of barely a dozen buildings. One was a stable, another a small general store. The midday heat had driven everyone indoors, and the only sign of life as Nate led his party down the dusty street was a yellow mongrel lying under an overhang. The dog raised its head, stared a bit, and went back to sleep.

The hitch rail in front of the general store was empty. Nate wrapped the bay's reins around the rail and stretched to relieve a kink in his back. "We'll rest here an hour or so."

"Why so long, sir?" Samuel Worth asked. "The sooner we reach the mountains, the happier me and my family will be."

"There's no sense in wearing out our horses," Nate replied. "We have a long way to go yet."

Emala awkwardly dismounted and smoothed her dress. She squinted up at the sun, then scanned the street from end to end. "If we have to stop we have to stop. But I don't like bein' out in the open like this. We should find us a shady spot to rest."

"There's a big tree over by the stable, Ma," Randa mentioned. "We could sit in the shade."

"Good idea, daughter," Samuel said. He started off but turned to Nate. "Give a holler when you are ready to go and we will come on the run."

"A walk will do," Nate said. He stayed by the hitch rail, watching them. His suspicion had flared anew, and he debated what to do.

"Is something the matter, husband?" Winona asked. "You have a troubled look about you."

"How is it you can read my mind like I can read an open book?" Nate responded.

"We have been together many winters," Winona said with affection. "I would be a poor excuse for a woman if I could not read your moods."

"So you're saying it's a special trait you females have?" Nate teased.

"If by trait you mean love, yes. When a woman cares for a man, she wants to please him in every way she can. Since men keep so much inside, she must look for little things he does that tell her how he is feeling. You have always been very open with me but there are still times I must read you, as you put it."

Nate felt a prick of conscience. "I guess I should have told you sooner, then."

"Told me what?"

"That the Evans family are runaway slaves."

Winona stared after them. She had heard about how whites used blacks to till fields and do other work, and she knew that slavery was widespread. The idea that people were treated like that had always appalled her. "What makes you think so? Because they are black?"

"Give me more credit," Nate said. "Haven't you noticed how skittish they are? And didn't it strike you as strange that all they own are the clothes on their backs and horses better fit to pull a plow?"

"So you are saying they must be slaves because they are poor?"

"I've never heard of rich slaves. But no, it's how they act. If I'm right, we're breaking the law by helping them."

Winona had never understood why whites needed so many laws. It was almost as if they could not live in peace without them. Her people did not have laws. Each Shoshone was responsible for his or her own conduct, and was expected to behave as was best for the good of all. "What do you suggest we do?" White laws meant nothing to her. But she had learned the hard way that they applied to her family whether she wanted them to or not. Her son, Zach, was once arrested and put on trial for killing white men, and came close to being hanged.

"For the moment, nothing." Nate didn't mind helping them. He had been raised in New York, which abolished slavery long before he was born. And personally, he thought it wrong for one man to lord it over another. But he didn't like that Lester Evans wasn't being honest with him. Then again, Evans might be afraid he would turn them in.

At that moment a man came out of the general store. A smudged white apron covered his ample middle, and his moon face glistened with sweat. "I tell you, if there is anywhere on God's green earth more humid than Missouri, I have yet to hear of it." He smiled and held out a pudgy hand. "Orville Barstow is my name. I saw you folks ride in out my window."

Nate shook his hand.

"Anything I can help you with, anything you need, let me know." Orville gave Winona an appreciative glance. "A frontiersman, I take it? And this must be your squaw."

Nate almost hit him. He started to ball his fist, but Winona's hand found his wrist. "She is my wife. Call her that again and I'll gut you."

Orville blinked and swallowed. "Sorry, mister. I didn't mean no insult. It's just what folks hereabouts call Injun women, is all." He forced another smile and his gaze drifted toward the stable. "Are those darkies yours, too?"

"You ask a lot of questions."

"I'm only being sociable." Orville wiped his hands on his apron. "This here is Barstow's Corner. Named after my grandpa. The store has been in our family three generations now."

Nate would as soon punch him for the way he had looked at Winona, and what he called her. But he controlled his temper and said, "Not many people about."

"Not at this time of day, no. By evening some of the farmers will drift in and gather around my cracker barrel. And on Sundays we always have a social at the church. The ladies gossip and the men eat until they are fit to burst." Orville waited, and when Nate didn't say anything, he moved toward his store. "Well, like I said, if you need anything, anything at all, I'm the man to see." The door closed behind him.

"You should have let me hit him," Nate said.

"How much money do we have left in our poke?" Winona asked.

Under the circumstances, Nate thought her question peculiar, and said so, adding, "We have all the ammunition and salt and flour we need."

"I was not thinking of us." Winona motioned toward the stable. "They need flour and sugar and a few other things. A knife, perhaps. Or a pistol. Or even a rifle if this store has any for sale."

Nate pursed his lips. Guns weren't cheap. A common Kentucky rifle cost upwards of fifteen dollars. A pistol could be had for less, but there was the ammo to buy, and the powder, and the patches.

"What else should we get them?" Winona went on. "A fire steel and flint, maybe, so they can start fires. And an axe so they can fell trees for their cabin."

Nate frowned. Fire steels were cheap enough but an axe could cost three dollars or more. Add the cost of a pistol and possibly a rifle, and he came to the conclusion that, "You intend to spend every last cent we have left on them, don't you?"

"They are in need but are too proud to ask for our help."

"The more we help them, the more trouble we can get into if they're runaways and we get caught."

"Then you will have to see to it that we don't."

"Do you realize what you're asking? I might have to shoot someone."

"Would *you* want to be a slave?"

"It's an awful lot for us to do for people we hardly know," Nate said. "But I'll do it if you insist."

Winona rose onto her toes and kissed him on the cheek. "Do I really need to?"

"You don't fight fair."

"No woman ever does."

"What do you suppose they're talkin' about?" Emala wondered. She was sitting with her back to the elm and her hands folded in her lap.

"I'm sure I have no idea," Samuel said. He had more important things on his mind. It was beginning to dawn on him that maybe, just maybe, they would pull it off, that they would reach the Rockies and never need to worry about being caught and dragged back to Georgia. "We should have seen sign of them by now," he said half under his breath.

"What? Sign of who?"

"The slave chasers. It's been weeks. Maybe they lost our trail. Maybe we're in the clear and frettin' over nothin'."

"Or it could be they'll show up any day now," Emala said. She had learned long ago to always expect the worst.

"If you were the sky you would always be cloudy," Samuel criticized. He stretched out on his back and closed his eyes.

Randa was tired of them spatting. They never fought this much before they fled the plantation. To change the subject, she asked, "Pa, how dangerous will it be in the mountains?"

Chickory grinned. He had stuck a blade of grass in his mouth and was idly plucking others out of the ground. "We'll need eyes in the backs of our heads, what with all the mountain lions and bears and Indians."

"Don't be tryin' to scare your sister," Emala said. "We had cougars and bears back home."

"Black bears," Chickory said. "They ain't nothin' like grizzlies."

"How would you know?"

Samuel opened his eyes. "The boy is right. I've done some askin' around. Grizzlies are twice as big and ten times as mean. The mountain lions are bigger, too, but they fight shy of folks."

"And the Indians?" Randa said.

"Some are nice and some ain't. You heard about York. He gets along fine with the Crows. And Mr.

King was adopted by the Shoshones. What we need is to find us a friendly tribe and live with them or near them and we'll do all right."

"There won't be any other black folks, though, will there?" Emala asked. "It will be us and only us."

"There's York."

"And we won't ever see our kin and our friends again, will we?"

"We don't dare ever go back, no."

A terrible sadness came over Emala. It wasn't that she didn't love her family. She loved them more than anything. But to be by themselves way up in those horrid mountains would fill her with loneliness for more of her own kind. She liked a lot of people around. She liked to have friends around. She liked to have other women to talk to. And what about Randa and Chickory? she wondered. There would be no one their age for them to have fun with. It was enough to make her weep, but instead she began to hum to herself to try and raise her spirits. Before long she was softly singing one of her favorite songs. "Swing low, sweet chariot, comin' for to carry me home. . . ."

Samuel smiled. His wife had a good voice. He loved to sit and listen to her sing by the hour. He often joined in, as he did now. ". . . Swing low, sweet chariot, comin' for to carry me home. . . ."

Randa always sang at the plantation services and knew the words as well as they did. ". . . I looked over Jordan and what did I see, comin' for to carry me home, a band of angels comin' after me, comin' for to carry me home. . . ." She nudged her brother with her toe.

Chickory shook his head. He only sang because his parents made him. But when his sister wouldn't stop nudging him, he reluctantly gave in. ". . . . Swing low, sweet chariot, comin' for to carry me home. . . ."

Warm memories flooded through Emala. Memories of the many happy times they had before they fled. She sang louder and the others followed her lead. The air was hot and still, the town quiet and tranquil, and for a short while Emala forgot where they were and why they were there. She was at peace with the world for the first time in weeks. After they finished the first song, she launched into "Rock of Ages."

A few heads poked out of doors and a woman opened an upstairs window and leaned out to hear better.

Emala sang at full volume, as if by singing she could make things right again. If she could, she would banish all the bad in the world and make it so that everyone, black and white, lived free and happy, and no one ever had to call anyone else master.

Hardly pausing for breath, Emala began a third song. "Steal away, steal away, steal away to Jesus. . . ."

Samuel, Randa and Chickory merged in perfect harmony.

". . . Steal away, steal away home, I ain't got long to stay here. My lord he calls me, he calls me by the thunder. . . ."

More people came outside to listen. Some smiled and tapped their feet. A few frowned and made remarks.

Emala ignored the mean ones. She was tired of mean people, tired of those who couldn't see past the color of a person's skin. To her way of thinking it was downright silly. God made blacks and God made whites and God made the red man, too, and if those colors were all right by God, then by God, they should be all right by those people God made those colors. She would show them through her singing how foolish they were. She would show that there was goodness and beauty in all folks, and all they had to do was open their hearts to it.

"Let's do another, Ma," Randa said when "Steal Away" ended.

" 'Deep River,' " Emala said, and the words flowed from her in a musical stream of perfect pitch. "Deep river, my home is over Jordan. Deep river, Lord, I want to cross over into campground. . . ."

Some of the listeners came nearer and an older man timidly joined in, his voice crackling like dry sticks.

". . . . Oh, don't you want to go to that Gospel feast, that promised land where all is peace? Oh, don't you want to go to that promised land, that land where all is peace? Deep river, my home is over Jordan. Deep river, Lord, I want to cross over into campground."

Emala stopped, and everyone stopped with her. She couldn't see for the tears in her eyes or sing for the lump in her throat.

"Are you all right, woman?" Samuel asked.

Coughing, Emala said softly, "I'll never be all right again."

Chapter Fifteen

Catfish had a reputation as one of the best slave catchers in the business. He had been at it for years. He was good because he was crafty; he had a knack for outthinking his quarry. He always planned ahead, he never took chances he didn't need to, and he relied on the element of surprise. Usually he took them alive. Not that he gave a damn whether they lived or died. It was just that invariably he was paid more if they were breathing, and Catfish was powerfully fond of money.

Once Catfish figured out that his latest prey was making for the frontier, his job became easier. Of all the roads out of St. Louis, most travelers bound for St. Joseph and the fringe of civilization took what some called the St. Joe road. He and his men pushed hard but were careful not to ride their animals into the ground. Without horses they might as well give up.

Now and then they stopped to ask if others had seen any sign of a black family. Several freighters were the first to say that they had, in company with what one of the freighters described as "a mountain of a man in buckskins and a pretty peach of an Injun gal."

Catfish grew excited. He loved the thrill of the chase. As a boy he had loved to hunt and been uncommonly good at it. It was only natural that when he grew up he looked for work that suited his passion. Hunting slaves was made to order.

As more travelers confirmed that they were closing in on the Worths, Catfish could practically hear the money for their capture clinking as he counted it. But he also became cautious. As he put it when he and his men stopped to rest their horses, "I don't like this business about a mountain man and his squaw."

"What difference does it make?" Pickett asked. "There are five of us and only one of him."

"The squaw doesn't hardly count," Trumbo rumbled.

"Now, see," Catfish said, putting his hands on his hips and regarding them with annoyance, "this is why you work for me and not the other way around. Not a one of you use your damn heads for anything more than a hat rack."

"Here now," Wesley said. "I didn't say a word, did I? Fact is, I agree. Mountain men aren't weak sisters. They're tough and they can be terrible mean when riled. And a squaw will slit a man's throat as quick as a buck."

Catfish nodded in satisfaction. Of them all, buckskin-clad Wesley was the best backwoodsman and the one most likely to see his point. "What we have to do is jump them, not give them a chance to draw a weapon."

"Criminy, why go to all that bother?" young Joe Earl complained. "We have the right to shoot anyone who tries to stop us. You said so yourself."

"That's as it should be, boy," Catfish said. "But the

trick is to not get shot ourselves. This mountain man worries me."

"So how do you suggest we go about it?" Pickett asked.

Catfish already had that worked out. When they met a farmer in a wagon who told them that yes, he had seen a family of four blacks in Barstow's Corner, which wasn't half a mile down the road, Catfish had his men wait while he rode on alone. He held his horse to a walk so it wouldn't be lathered with sweat and give the impression he had been riding hard. As he neared the hamlet he plastered a smile on his face and whistled as if he didn't have a care in the world.

The stable was the first building Catfish came to, and he nearly gave himself away. For there, sitting in the shade of a tall tree, were the four he was after. He deliberately pretended to ignore them and rode on by. Drawing rein in front of the general store, he swung down and was tying his horse off when the door opened and out came the mountain man and the Indian woman. There could be no doubt it was them. They fit the descriptions he had been given right down to the white feather the mountain man wore.

Catfish ignored them, too. He made a show of poking about in a saddlebag as if looking for something.

The pair stopped a few yards away. The mountain man was holding a burlap bag that bulged with whatever they bought.

"Well, I hope you are happy."

"I am, husband. We are doing the right thing."

"We're just about broke."

"It is not like you to quibble. We have more money at home. Come. We will show the Evanses what we bought for them."

Catfish went into the store. He shammed an interest in a shelf of tools and watched out the front window as the pair crossed to the stable. The mention of the Evanses puzzled him. The four blacks were named Worth. It must be, he reasoned, that the slaves were using different names. And if that was the case, likely as not they hadn't told the mountain man who they were really were, or that they were on the run. Which worked in his favor, since now the mountain man wouldn't be expecting trouble.

Catfish picked up a hammer and hefted it as if testing how heavy it was. He saw the mountain man set down the burlap sack. The Indian woman—and God Almighty, she was as fine a woman of any color that Catfish ever saw—opened it and proceeded to hand a pistol to Samuel Worth.

Catfish scowled. Damn them to hell and back, he thought. Armed slaves nearly always made a fight. Fortunately, few ever got their hands on a gun. But this didn't bode well. Nor did he like it when the mountain man gave Samuel Worth a knife. "Son of a bitch."

"I beg your pardon?"

Catfish gave a start. An old biddy in a blue bonnet was by the dry goods, her thin face pinched in distaste. "Ma'am?"

"Watch your language around a lady. I don't put up with that from my Harold, and I damn well won't put up with it from a stranger."

"My apologies, ma'am," Catfish said, when he would just as soon hit her with the hammer.

The biddy sniffed, then said, "That's some accent you have. Where are you from, if you don't mind my asking?"

"Georgia," Catfish said. Lying wouldn't serve any purpose.

"You're a long way from home." She came over and gazed out the window. "We get all kinds in Barstow's Corner these days."

"I didn't know you were standing there when I cussed," Catfish said.

"Oh, I didn't mean you," the biddy responded. She was staring in the direction of the stable. "You're rude, but at least you are white. We see too many of *their* kind."

"Ma'am?"

"You have eyes, don't you? We can do without the likes of those blacks and that red yonder."

"You don't care for Indians, ma'am?"

"I should say not. My grandfather was killed by red devils. And that one!" The biddy sniffed. "She walked in here as fancy as you please. And you should have heard her, talking as white as anyone."

"Any idea what tribe she's from?"

"I honestly don't care. Red is red. But I gather from what little I heard that they're bound for the Rockies. Good riddance to red trash and those who associate with red trash, I say."

The biddy walked off. Catfish put down the hammer and gave a scythe a test swing. The whole time he was thinking he must be mighty careful how he went about capturing the Worths. Mighty careful indeed. Because if the mountain man and his red filly were buying things for the Worths, they weren't about to stand for him slapping chains on them.

Catfish was about to leave when he realized it might seem suspicious, him walking out with nothing. Not that the Worths or the mountain man had paid any attention to him. But he always played it smart. Accordingly, he went to the counter and bought coffee.

Catfish made it a point not to glance toward the stable as he stepped into the stirrups. As he rode off, he could see them out of the corner of his eye, the mountain man and his woman, smiling and friendly with the blacks. If the pair gave him trouble when the time came, it was just too bad for them. Five thousand dollars was five thousand dollars. For that much he would turn them into maggot bait with no regrets.

The basic law of surviving in the wilderness was simple: the alert and the quick lived; the dull and the slow died. Nate King had learned the lesson quickly and survived. Other trappers never learned it and never came back from the mountains.

The only time Nate let down his guard was in the safety and security of his cabin. The moment he stepped out that door, he cast off his sense of well-being and became instead as wary and alert as an animal. The flutter of a butterfly, the sweep of a bird's wings, the swift bound of a rabbit, nothing escaped him.

So it was that the arrival of the short man in homespun clothes, with more arms than an arsenal, didn't go unnoticed. The moment Nate and Winona stepped out of the general store, Nate spotted him. That the man made a point of not looking at them perked his curiosity. Nate watched the man without being obvious and was willing to swear the man was doing the same.

The Evans family, though, hardly gave the man a glance.

Which puzzled Nate. He began to think that maybe he was mistaken. Maybe his hunch was wrong. He remarked to Winona that he should come right out and ask the Evanses if they were escaped slaves but she thought it best not to.

"Let them do it in their own good time. When they trust us enough, they will."

They were an hour out of Barstow's Corner when Nate thought the moment had come. Samuel Worth brought his mount up next to Nate's bay and paced it, saying, "There's somethin' I'd like to say to you, Mr. King."

"How many times must I remind you? Call me Nate or call me Grizzly Killer."

"Grizzly what?"

"Grizzly Killer. It's the name the Indians know me by."

"You don't say. I'll try, but old habits are hard to break." Samuel pulled the brim of his floppy hat lower over his eyes to ward off the harsh glare of the sun. "It's about all the things you and your lady gave us."

Nate liked how he referred to Winona. "You've already thanked us. What more is there?"

"Thankin' ain't enough," Samuel said. He couldn't get over how kind the Kings were. The pistol wedged snug under his belt and the knife on his hip were possessions beyond compare. "You see, no one has ever treated us this decent before."

"There are a lot of nice folks in the world."

"That there are. But nice ain't always enough. We've been treated nice by some folks who wouldn't lift a finger to help us if we were in trouble." Samuel caressed his new flintlock. "I don't know as how I will ever be able to pay you back."

"It's a gift, Lester. You don't repay gifts."

Conscience pricked Samuel. He shouldn't go on living a lie, he told himself. He opened his mouth to reveal the truth but couldn't do it. It made him feel worse.

"You'll need what we gave you and a lot more if you're to last six months in the high country," Nate cautioned. "The most important thing is a rifle."

Samuel patted his pistol. "I reckon this will do."

"It's good enough to stop most anything at close range. But that's the problem. *Close* range. Most game won't be that obliging. To hunt, you really need a rifle."

"We'll get by," Samuel insisted.

"Not if you tangle with hostiles, you won't. With a rifle you can pick them off at a distance. Let them get near enough to use their bows and lances and you are done for."

"I hope to live where there ain't any hostiles. I don't want me and mine to have to look over our shoulders every time we step outside." Samuel paused. "You must know a place like that. Somewhere we could live in peace. Somewhere the bad Indians would leave us be."

"Heaven," Nate said.

"I'm serious, Mr. King."

"So am I. There's no place like that on earth. Anywhere you go in the mountains, there are friendly tribes and tribes that will kill you on sight. They'll kill you and yours and take your horses and leave your bodies for the buzzards."

"If you're tryin' to scare me it won't work."

Nate had met men like Lester Evans before. Deep down they were good and decent. But they couldn't get it through their heads that just because they were good, it didn't mean everyone was. They couldn't grasp that just because they didn't want to hurt anyone, others wouldn't want to hurt them.

"So you're sayin' it's hopeless?"

"The best you can hope for is to find a spot where hostiles rarely come, where there's enough game to last you a good many years, where there's water and graze for your horses."

"Well, do you know a place like *that*?"

Nate hesitated. He knew of one. The valley where he lived. King Valley, folks were calling it.

"You've got to understand, Mr. King. This is my chance to make somethin' of myself. To have my own land. To have my own roof over my head. To be more than I was before. I've got to make the best of it. Chances like this don't come along but once in a lifetime."

There was no denying his passion. But passion couldn't stop a barbed shaft or a lead ball. Nate remembered the old woman and her family, eager for a new life in Oregon Country. Look at where their passion got them.

Suddenly hooves clattered and Winona came up on his other side. "The two of you are done talking, husband."

"No, we're not," Nate said, surprised by her gall.

"That's all right," Samuel said.

"You are done talking."

Nate arched an eyebrow. "What on earth has gotten into you?"

"We are being followed."

Chapter Sixteen

They halted on the crest of the next hill.

From their vantage point the road was a dusty serpent that wound off through the lush Missouri greenery. Half a mile back riders had appeared. With the riders were several four-footed creatures other than horses. Nate studied them through his spyglass. "Dogs," he announced. "Bloodhounds. Three, plus four men."

"Sweet Jesus," Emala said. Her worst fear had come to pass. She clasped her hands and rolled her eyes to the heavens. "Save us, please. Don't let them hang my Samuel."

"Your who?" Winona asked.

"Maybe they're not after us, Ma," Randa said without conviction. "They could be anybody."

Winona, eyeing Emala quizzically, answered the daughter with, "They have been following us since we left Barstow's Corner."

Still peering through the spyglass, Nate recognized the lead rider. It was the short man who paid the hamlet a visit shortly before they rode out. He folded the telescope and slid it into one of the parfleches tied to his bay. "They're about an hour behind. My guess is they'll wait until we camp for the night, then close in." He shifted in the saddle. "So your real name is Samuel, I take it? Don't you reckon it's time you told us the truth?"

His hand on the pistol the Kings gave him, Samuel grimaced with embarrassment. "You know, then?"

"I know," Nate King said. He looked at each of them in turn.

Emala met his level gaze. "We're sorry, Mr. King. As God is my witness, we didn't want to deceive you. But we've been on the run for so long, never knowin' when they would come after us—" Choked with emotion, Emala broke off.

Winona reined her horse closer and leaned over to place a hand on the other woman's arm. "It is all right. We are friends."

"No, it's not all right," Emala said, shaking her head. "We lied to you. And lyin' is sinful." She let out a sob. "After you've been so nice to us, too."

"We're escaped slaves," Samuel admitted, and felt an invisible weight rise from his shoulders. "Those men back there are slave hunters. They make their livin' trackin' down folks like us and takin' us back to our masters to be punished."

"We ain't ever goin' back!" Randa said heatedly. "I won't let them hang my pa for helpin' me."

Samuel had to cough to clear his throat. "Mr. King, it might be best if you and Mrs. King went on by yourselves. This is our problem. We'll deal with it as best we can."

"Suppose you tell us all there is," Nate said, "and let us decide about the dealing."

"I can't ask you to mix in," Samuel said. "Those men won't stop at nothin'. They'll hurt you if you take our side. Hurt you or worse."

Winona said again, "You are our friends."

"I guess I have to."

While Emala softly wept, Samuel unburdened his soul. He told it straight and simple, concluding with, "And that's how we came to run. I didn't mean to kill Master Brent, but I couldn't let him put his hands on my girl. I just couldn't."

Nate thought of Evelyn, and how he would feel if a man tried to force himself on her. "I'd have done the same. Only it wouldn't have been an accident."

"You would?"

"No son of a bitch tries to rape my daughter and gets away with it," Nate said grimly.

Chickory laughed.

"Husband," Winona scolded. She agreed, though. She would defend her loved ones however she needed to. Among her people the men were the warriors, but the women were expected to help defend the village when enemies raided.

Nate had come to a decision. "My wife is right, Samuel. You're our friends. We can't let them take you."

"But if you help us, it'll put you on the wrong side of the law."

"I've been on the wrong side before." The law, Nate had found, was often perverted by those who twisted it to their own ends. Supposedly everyone was entitled to fair treatment, but those with money could buy fairness like people bought groceries.

Winona had lived with her man long enough to know what he would do in situations like this. "We will send the Worths on ahead and you and I will stop these slave hunters."

Nate crooked his mouth in a smirk. She didn't fool him. "You go with Samuel and his family. Ride hard and fast. I'll catch up when I can."

"Not by yourself," Winona said.

"There are only four. I'll discourage them without taking life, if I can." Nate lifted his reins. "Don't dally. I need to find a spot to make my stand."

Samuel had listened to their exchange in some amazement. "Hold on, sir. I can't let you do this. It's our fight, not yours. And those men back there, they're awful good at what they do. You might think you have an edge, livin' in the wild as you do, but some of them are bound to be backwoods boys, and they have their dogs."

"I've fought Blackfeet and Sioux," Nate said confidently. "Not to mention Comanches and Apaches. Compared to them, four Georgians should be easy."

"It ain't right."

"We should do as Mr. King wants," Emala said. "He knows best."

"Hush, woman."

Nate reined his bay broadside across the road. "We can sit here and argue while they get closer and put your whole family in danger. Or you can light a shuck and repay me later."

"Repay how?" Samuel shook his head. "There's no repayin' a thing like this." Reluctantly, he kneed his horse. He looked back several times, and the mountain man was still there. "Your man sure is special," he remarked to Winona.

"It is why I married him."

"Ain't you worried?" Emala asked. "Even a little bit?"

"He can take care of himself," Winona said. But

she *was* worried. It was one against four. Plus the bloodhounds.

"God help him," Emala Worth said.

Catfish and the others were strung out in single file and almost to a bend when young Joe Earl came galloping out of the woods and brought his sweaty horse to a sliding stop. "What set your britches on fire, boy?"

Joe Earl mopped his brow with a sleeve, then said excitedly, "I've been doin' like you told me, followin' them but stayin' off the road. They had no notion I was there."

"You came all the way back to tell me that?" Catfish didn't entirely trust the youth's judgment. He'd only hired him because he was his wife's cousin, and if he hadn't, she would have made his life miserable.

"They know we're after them!" Joe Earl exclaimed.

"Hell," Trumbo rumbled.

Catfish motioned. "Calm down, boy. Tell us exactly what you saw." He listened to how the mountain man had used a spyglass and what happened after. "So the Injun gal and the darkies went on ahead, did they?" He thoughtfully scratched the stubble on his chin. "That mountain man thinks he's bein' clever, but we can be clever too. Yes, sir. This has possibilities."

"That it does," Wesley agreed, the stock of his Kentucky rifle resting on his buckskin-clad leg. "We can be as tricky as he can."

Turning, Catfish opened a saddlebag and took out a gleaming bronze tube. He held it out to Pickett. "Take this spyglass and shimmy up that tall tree. Find out what the mountain man is up to. Don't let yourself be seen."

"Why me?" Pickett objected.

"Because I said so." Catfish never was fond of toads, four-legged or otherwise. But Pickett had a trait that made him invaluable; he would kill anyone or anything. Man, woman, kid, kitten, it didn't matter.

"Dammit," Pickett groused. But he took the spyglass and hurried to the tree. For a human toad he was remarkably agile and climbed swiftly to a fork sixty feet up. There, he braced his back against the trunk and raised the spyglass to his right eye. "I can see him!" he called down.

"Yell a little louder so he can hear you."

"We're too far off," Pickett said, then glanced down and realized Catfish was joshing. "You're not as hilarious as you think you are." He raised the telescope again. "The mountain man is still there. He's just sittin' on his horse in the middle of the road."

"Is he lookin' our way through his spyglass?"

"What? No. His hands are empty. Well, except for reins. Wait. He's movin'. Looks like he goin' off into the trees on the north side of the road."

"Be sure it's the north side," Catfish said.

"Hell, I'm not no simpleton. I can tell north from south, and he's goin' to the north."

"All right. Come on down. And don't drop my spyglass or you'll buy me a new one."

Joe Earl was so worked up he could hardly sit his saddle. "What do we do now? Go kill the mountain man and then light out after his squaw and the blacks?"

Catfish gave a snort of amusement. "Boy, you beat all. You want us to tangle with that he-bear?"

"There are five of us and one of him," Joe Earl said. "Or we could set the hounds on him and have them rip him to pieces like they did that painter a while back."

Wesley laughed.

"What's so blamed funny?" Joe Earl demanded.

"You are, boy," Catfish said. "You ain't got the brains God gave a squirrel. Why go up against that mountain man if we don't have to? I saw him up close, and he's loaded for bear and then some. A Hawken, pistols, a bowie. And you can bet the farm he's damn deadly with all of them."

"But—" Joe Earl began.

Catfish raised a hand. "I ain't done. One of the reasons I've lasted so long in this business is I never take chances when there's no need. Take that mountain man. He's likely waitin' over yonder for us to come waltzin' by so he can pick us off. Or maybe all he intends is to take our horses and guns and strand us afoot. But he's in for a surprise. We're goin' to outsmart the bastard."

"How?"

"I swear," Catfish said in disgust. "Everyone mount up. We have us some ridin' to do." As an afterthought he said, "And Trumbo, you keep those dogs quiet, you hear? I don't want them bayin' and givin' us away."

An hour was all it took. First they entered the woods on the south side of the road and rode for a quarter of a mile, far enough in that no one on the road, or near it, would hear them when, as they soon did, they turned west and paralleled the road for more than a mile. By then they were well past the mountain man. Swinging north, they returned to the road and took up the chase anew.

"That was mighty slick, cousin," Joe Earl said.

"Slick beats stupid all hollow. It's worth rememberin'." Catfish imagined the mountain man's reaction when he discovered he'd been outfoxed, and chuckled.

They held to a gallop, the bloodhounds loping beside Trumbo's horse with that rolling gait they had, their long ears flapping and their tongues lolling.

Clods of dirt told Catfish that the woman and the slaves were moving fast. But he doubted they would go far, not with the Indian woman's man back there. Catfish had seen how she looked at the man back at Barstow's Corner, seen the love in her eyes as plain as if she were wearing a sign. No, a woman like that would only leave her man because the man made her, and then she wouldn't go far in case he needed her.

A hill rose ahead, the highest since St. Louis. Catfish slowed to spare the horses and the dogs. It occurred to him that the top of the hill was a good spot for the woman and the blacks to wait, but they weren't there. Drawing rein, he informed the others, "We'll rest a few minutes."

"I'll ride on ahead and see where the others got to," Wesley offered. He started down the other side, but he only went a short way before drawing rein.

"Change your mind?" Catfish asked.

Holding on to his saddle, Wesley swung low to the ground and intently studied the tracks. "I'll be damned." He swung up, reined around, and came back to the top. He moved along the south edge of road for about thirty feet, then reined to the north side and rode along the edge, abruptly stopping where the trees were thinnest. "Get the dogs to sniffin'."

"What have you found?"

Wesley pointed. "They must have seen us and taken to the woods."

Catfish hurried over. Sure enough, fresh tracks pointed off into the trees. Sudden alarm spread through him. "Shake a leg with those hounds, Trumbo. The Injun's likely to be headin' back to her mountain man."

Trumbo climbed down and brought the bloodhounds over. Their long noses to the ground, they roved back and forth until the biggest uttered a *woof* and raised his head. Big Red, he was called, the most dependable of the three. The other two, both with tan coats, were identical enough to be twins. General Jackson and Boone were their names. Quickly, Trumbo undid the leash from each of their collars. Stepping back, he raised an arm. "Do I give the word?"

"If you don't, I'll shoot you." Catfish always thrilled to the release of the dogs. He liked to use three because one or even two might lose a scent, but he had never had three lose one. His were specially trained by a Savannah breeder considered the best in the business. Catfish paid extra so that his hounds, unlike most of their good-natured kin, would attack on command.

"Find!" Trumbo roared.

With a low bray from Big Red, they were gone.

Catfish forked leather and raised his reins. "Remember, we want the darkies alive."

"What about the Injun woman?" Pickett asked.

"Her we make a good Injun." Catfish chortled. "After we've had our fun."

Chapter Seventeen

Winona King had stopped on top of the hill to wait for Nate. He'd told her to keep pushing west and he would catch up after he dealt with the slave hunters. But her heart would not her let her run off and leave him. Nor would her upbringing; Shoshone women stuck by their men in times of trial.

Winona loved Nate, loved him as deeply as any woman ever loved any man. That he was white and she was red had absolutely no bearing on their bond. He was her man and she was his woman and they would be together until the day they died. That was how she looked at it, and if this was that day, then so be it.

So Winona stopped on top of the high hill. She informed the Worths that they would stay there until Nate rejoined them, and they settled down to wait. Winona knew they had come too far to hear shots or screams or the howls of the hounds, but she listened anyway. She listened and she watched the road, and so it was that she spotted the slave hunters the moment they broke from the trees on the south side of the road.

Winona's blood froze in her veins. The slave men had outsmarted her husband. Now it was up to her to save the Worths. But how, against five men and their bloodhounds?

Emala felt faint when she saw the road fill with riders and dogs. "Dear Lord!" she exclaimed. "Is there no end to this nightmare? They'll catch us now, as sure as I'm standin' here."

"Not without a fight they won't," Samuel vowed, his hands on his new weapons. He would give as good an account of himself as he could. "Maybe it's best this way."

"Samuel Worth, you're sun struck."

"I'm tired of runnin', woman. I'm tired of livin' in fear. It's time to end it, one way or the other."

"I don't like the other," Emala said.

Winona swung on to her sorrel. "We must ride, and ride hard. We will try to reach my husband before those slave men reach us."

Samuel didn't argue. As much as he wanted to end it, he would spare his family if he could. "You heard the lady."

Winona led them into the forest on the north side of the road. She wound through the thick trees and heavy brush with a skill born of long experience on horseback. But her new friends weren't as experienced. They went slower, and she refused to desert them.

They had been at it a while when a throaty bray warned them the chase had begun in earnest.

"They've set the hounds on us!" Randa exclaimed.

"Give me your knife, Pa, and I'll help you fight," Chickory offered.

"Just ride, the both of you," Samuel said. "Ride as you've never ridden before."

The futility gnawed at Winona. There was no way they could escape. The slave hunters had good horses, were undoubtedly better riders, and they had their dogs. She began to cast about for somewhere to make a stand. Not a minute later they emerged into a clearing and she immediately drew rein.

"Why did we stop?" Samuel asked, his wide eyes fixed on the woods behind them. The dogs were coming, and he feared dogs more than he feared just about anything.

"This is where we part company. I will stay and stop them. You will take your family and keep going until you reach Nate."

Randa blinked. "You want us to run out on you?"

"You can do little unarmed," Winona pointed out. "And saving all of you is what is important."

Emala's chest filled with warmth, despite her terror. "You're the best friend anyone could ever want."

"Get them out of here," Winona urged. "We do not have much time."

Samuel was torn between flight and fight. He glanced from Winona to his family and back again. The choice was simple, really. "My family always comes first or I wouldn't do this."

"I understand," Winona assured him, and motioned. "Hurry. I think I hear the dogs."

Samuel didn't hear anything but he took her word for it. "Do as she says," he commanded.

Chickory scowled, but used his heels. Randa followed after him. Emala, her eyes brimming with tears, tried to say something and couldn't. She kneed her horse on.

"I'm sorry we brought this on you," Samuel said.

Winona climbed down. "Are you still here? Your family will need you if they get past me." The right word was "when," but she could not bring herself to say it.

"Thank you."

The clomp of hooves faded. Winona hid in the vegetation at the edge of the clearing, the stock of her rifle pressed to her shoulder, the hammer back and the trigger set. She thought of Nate and ached inside, and then there was no time for anything except staying alive.

The three bloodhounds burst into the clearing. They made no more noise than the breeze save for their sniffing. Heads down, tails up, they roved about the spot where Winona and the Worths had stopped.

Winona sighted on the red one. She had no qualms about killing animals, and these had to be killed if the Worths were to live. Still, when the hound raised its great head and looked straight at her, she hesitated for the briefest instant. Enough for the red hound to bray a warning and for all three to break for cover.

Winona fired. The ball caught the red hound high in the neck and the hound went down, wailing with pain. The other two made it to cover before Winona could unlimber a pistol. She backed toward her horse, every sense alert, but she failed to hear the pad of heavy paws until they were almost on top of her. She whirled just as one of the tan hounds sprang. Her pistol went off in its face. The impact bowled her over and she lost her hold on her rifle. She started to rise just as the third dog was on her.

Slavering jaws snapped at Winona's throat. She jerked back and clubbed the hound with her spent pistol. Hitting its thick skull was like hitting a tree stump, and had no more effect. The hound snapped at her wrist and its fangs tore her sleeve.

Winona groped for her other pistol. She had her

hand on it when the bloodhound bit at her leg. Springing aside, she tripped over a bush and lost her balance. The next instant she was on her side and the hound was above her, poised to rip and rend. Its maw gaped; its fangs glistened.

The blast of a shot and the bursting of the dog's eyeball were simultaneous. It collapsed on top of her, dead, and she pushed it off of her so she could sit up. "You should not have come back."

"They refused to leave you," Samuel said, smoke curling from the muzzle of his new pistol. He had held it close to the dog's head so as not to miss. "What else could I do?"

Emala, Randa and Cickory sat their horses a dozen feet away. Emala said, "I couldn't live with myself, runnin' off on you like that."

Samuel offered his big hand and helped Winona up. "Do we fight here or do we run?"

"We run." With the hounds dead, Winona had a good chance of losing the slave hunters. She scooped up her rifle and stepped to the sorrel. As she was pulling herself up, Emala screamed.

"Look out!"

A rider crashed out of the undergrowth, a lanky man in buckskins who held his rifle by the barrel. He was on Samuel as Samuel turned. The thud of the hardwood stock striking Samuel's head was sickeningly loud.

Winona spun. In a twinkling the man in buckskins reined toward her. She tried to dodge, but the stock caught her across the shoulder and she was sent to her knees in a flood of pain.

Practically flying from his saddle, the man reversed his grip on his Kentucky long gun and trained it on her, growling at the stunned Worths,

"Any of you so much as twitch and I'll send this squaw and your pa to hell."

The underbrush crackled and the other slave hunters poured out. Winona was tempted to use her pistol, but at least two more guns were centered on her; she would be dead before she got off a shot.

"We're caught, Ma!" Randa cried.

That they were.

"Well done, Wesley." Catfish hooked a leg over his saddle and stared in fury at the blacks and their Indian friend. "You killed our hounds, you bastards. For that you'll suffer, reward or no reward."

"I killed them," Winona accepted the blame to try to spare the Worths. "Do what you must with me, but leave them be."

"Ain't you the noble squaw," Catfish mocked her.

Pickett had leaped to the ground and was on his knees, holding Andrew Jackson's head in his lap. He swore luridly. "I say we kill her! She's nothin' to us. We kill her and we don't do it quick."

"I liked those critters," Trumbo rumbled.

"So did I." Catfish alighted and went over to Boone. Part of the hound's forehead had been blown off. "It won't be quick, squaw. You'll beg us to put you out of your misery before we're through. But first things first. Joe Earl, break out the manacles. We've got us some darkies to hobble."

"No!" To the astonishment of all, Chickory sprang down and flew at Wesley, his fists pinwheeling. "You're not takin' us back! I won't let you!"

The backwoodsman sidestepped. His moccasin-clad foot flicked out and down Chickory went, sprawling onto his hands and knees next to Samuel.

The boy lunged at his father, then rose brandishing his father's new blade.

Joe Earl pointed a rifle at him.

"No!" Emala screamed.

"No shootin'!" Catfish echoed her. "He's worth more alive, remember?"

Chickory stabbed at Wesley, but again the quicksilver backwoodsman evaded him with pantherish ease. A second time Chickory thrust, and yet a third. He was so intent on burying the blade in Wesley that he didn't hear a horse rein in close. The fist inkling he had of his peril was when his sister screamed his name. He looked up as Trumbo's rifle came sweeping down.

"Enough of this," Catfish said. "Get the manacles on and we will deal with the squaw."

Winona was inching her hand toward her other pistol. She intended to shoot the one who appeared to be the leader, then do what she could against the others. Suddenly a sharp prick between her shoulder blades turned her to stone.

"You're a sneaky bitch, ain't you?" Pickett snarled, and drove the knife in deep enough to draw a trickle of blood. "But you so much as touch that flintlock and I'll skin you alive."

Barking orders, Catfish had his men clap irons on Samuel and Chickory. Randa was hauled from her horse at gunpoint and subjected to the same indignity. Emala slid down on her own and wept softly as the leg irons were applied.

"Lord help us. It has come to this."

"What did you expect?" Catfish snapped. "Your man killed your master. Did you think Frederick Sullivan would let you get away scot-free?"

Emala sniffled.

"You brought this on yourselves. If it hadn't been us, it would be someone else come to drag you back. Your man has to pay, and you'll pay with him."

"The rest of us didn't do nothin'!" Randa defiantly responded.

"Oh? These horses you're ridin', you bought them, did you? Have a bill of sale to show the judge when we get back?" Catfish chortled. "We know you stole them. Damn near killed the wife of the farmer who owns them doin' it, too." He didn't hide his contempt. "You have a lot to answer for, gal." Catfish walked up to her, cupped her chin in his hand, and gave her a vicious shake. "From here on out you're not to give me sass. Not any, you hear?"

Randa spat in his face.

Enraged, Catfish flung her to the ground and kicked her in the stomach. "I'll teach you!" he fumed. "I'll teach you good." He unleashed a flurry of kicks.

Emala bawled for him to stop.

Curling into a ball, Randa held her arms over her head and took the punishment as best she could. She only cried out once, when his boot glanced off her ribs.

At last, puffing from exertion, Catfish lowered his foot and stepped back. "That's just a taste of what you'll get if you don't behave. I need you breathin', but I don't need you lively. Frederick Sullivan won't begrudge me a few bruises or a broken bone or two if you make a nuisance of yourself."

Emala let out a low sob. "Why are you doin' this to us?"

"That has to be the dumbest question I ever heard," Catfish said. "We do it for the money."

"Blood money."

"Call it what you want. It spends the same as any other kind." Catfish turned to Winona. "Now that the darkies are taken care of, it's your turn. Pickett, relieve the redskin of her weapons."

"My name is Winona." Winona's lower back was wet from the trickle of blood. She went to reach behind her but stopped when a rifle muzzle was flourished in her face.

"Don't move."

With no other recourse, Winona sought to stall them. "You would be wise to heed my advice and release us."

"My, don't you talk fancy," Catfish said. "But there is as much chance of that happenin' as there is a cow sproutin' wings."

"It would be for your own good. My husband will be on your trail soon."

"And that should worry us?" Catfish scoffed.

"You have seen him. To use your own words, does he look like the kind of man who will let you get away—how did you put it? Scot-free? Harm me, harm any of us, and he will come after you. He will hunt you down, however long it takes. There will be no stopping him, not this side of the grave."

Pickett raised his rifle over her head. "Want me to shut her up?"

Catfish scratched his stubble, thinking. "No. She's right. I've seen that husband of hers close up. He's not the kind to forgive and forget. He'll be out for our blood." Catfish smiled at Winona. "Thanks for the warnin', Injun. Let your man come. We'll be ready for him."

Chapter Eighteen

The life of a mountain man was not like the life of most men. Ordinary men could go about their ordinary lives oblivious to the world around them, and not come to harm. But a mountain man had to be alert every minute of every day. He had to be aware of everything that went on around him and be sensitive to the faintest disturbances. For it was often the little things—a sound, a scent, a hint of movement—that meant the difference between life and death.

Nate King made no claim to extraordinary senses. If asked, he would say his eyes, ears and nose were no better or worse than anyone else's. But years of wilderness living had honed his senses to razor sharpness. His hearing, in particular, was uncannily acute.

So it was that as Nate waited for the slave hunters to appear, the faintest of sounds pricked his ears. A sound so far off, so indistinct, he couldn't be sure he really heard it. But he would swear it was a shot.

Nate cocked his head and strained to hear another. The wind picked that moment to die. He went on listening for a while, but only the usual woodland noises were to be heard.

"I don't like this." Nate glanced over his shoulder

at the bay and voiced the thought that had been troubling him. "It's taking them too long."

The slave hunters should have shown by now.

Rising from concealment, Nate grasped the bay's reins and walked out to the road. It was empty save for a wagon well to the east. Opening the beaded parfleche, Nate took out his spyglass. In vain, he scoured the road and the forest fringing it for sign of them.

Suddenly that shot Nate thought he heard took on a whole new significance. Shoving the telescope back into the parfleche, Nate mounted, swung to the west, and used his heels to bring the bay to a gallop. As improbable as it seemed, the slave hunters must have gotten ahead of him. Since they didn't use the road, that meant they had cut through the woods. But why? The only answer he could think of was that they knew he was waiting for them. But that was impossible.

Nate shook his head in annoyance. He was thinking in circles. There was no way the slave men could have known he was lying in ambush. Unless—and at the insight, a chill ran through him—unless they had a spyglass of their own.

Nate grew sick inside at his lapse. He should have figured it out sooner.

The bay's hooves drumming, Nate tried not to worry. But Samuel had told him the Fugitive Slave Law gave the slave hunters the right to employ whatever force was necessary to take the fugitives into custody. That extended to lethal force, if need be.

Nate thought of the shot again, and said a single word under his breath. "Winona."

The fear for a loved one eclipses all others. It rips at the heart and throws the soul into turmoil. It can make a man reckless, and Nate rode recklessly now, pushing the bay even when the heat began to tell.

All Nate could think of was his wife. If she had tried to stop the slave hunters and they slew her, legally there was nothing he could do. Legally, he couldn't press charges and have them arrested and put on trial. Legally, they had the right to do as they needed.

To hell with the legality, Nate thought. If they harmed a hair on Winona's head, they would answer to him. If she was dead—and he couldn't bear to think that—then he would wipe the sons of bitches out and take whatever consequences befell him.

"Winona," Nate said again. The driving need to find her was overwhelming. In the distance, beyond a bend, a high hill loomed. From the top he would have a good view of the road ahead.

Then Nate swept around the bend, and the sight he beheld took a few seconds to sink in. He hauled on the reins, bringing the bay to a sliding halt, as consternation gripped him.

Ahead, in the middle of the road, was a woman on her knees, her head hung low. A woman with long black hair.

"Winona?" Nate said softly. She was several hundred yards away yet. Firming his grip on the Hawken, he gigged the bay. As he got closer he realized the woman's hands were bound behind her. Maybe her ankles were tied, too.

The woman looked up.

Pure, overpowering love pulsed through Nate. He almost rushed headlong to her rescue. Then he saw the gag, and his love was replaced by burning fury. Reining off the road into the woods on the north side, he swung down. The slave hunters thought they were being clever. Winona was bait, to lure him into their gun sights. But they were about to find out that they—

"Nate King!"

Hearing his name shouted was the last thing Nate expected.

"Nate King! I know you can hear me."

Nate cautiously crept to the edge of the trees but prudently didn't show himself. The man doing the shouting was standing next to Winona. It was the same man Nate had seen at Barstow's Corner, and he was holding a cocked pistol to Winona's head.

"Nate King! Either you answer me, or I will by God blow your squaw's brains out."

"I hear you!" Nate shouted.

The man smiled. "My name is Catfish. Me and my men have caught the runaways. Now we aim to take them back and collect the bounty."

Nate tried to read his wife's expression, but her hair was partially over her face.

"We don't want trouble with you, King. But you might take it into your head to side with the blacks, and we can't have that. So I've taken the liberty of trussin' your red missus up so we can parley."

"Parley?" Nate repeated.

"That's right. Why spill blood when we can talk this out? What do you say? Are you willin' to listen to reason?"

"All I care about is my wife." As Nate said it, he started forward, staying well hid.

"Then hear me out. What we propose is a trade. Your wife, for your word that you won't try to stop us. Now that's fair, ain't it?" Catfish did not wait for an answer. "We have the law on our side. We could kill her and you and be on our way. But you might get one or two of us. So I'd rather have your word of honor, instead. What do you say?"

Nate was moving as fast as he dared. He needed to be closer.

"Answer me, dammit. You're playin' with your wife's life. Or don't you care if I splatter her brains in the dirt?"

Nate cared, all right. *How* he cared! He responded, keeping his voice low and turning his head so Catfish would think he was farther away than he was. "I'm willing to talk."

Catfish's smiled widened. "Good. Good. Now suppose you show yourself and we can get this over with. All I want is your promise, and you can have her. Your promise and your weapons."

There it was. Nate was no fool. The second he handed over his rifle and pistols, the others would pop from cover and shoot him dead.

"What do you say, King? Be sensible. Do we have a deal?"

Cupping a hand over his mouth, Nate replied. "We have a deal!" He was almost to where he wanted to be.

"I like a man who can be reasoned with. All right, then. Show yourself and we'll get this over with."

Nate put on a last burst of speed, threading silently through the trees.

"King? Answer me, dammit. Don't try my patience or your woman is dead."

Near enough at last, Nate straightened and stepped into the open, holding the Hawken out from his side. His other hand was inches from his hip, and the butt of a flintlock. "Here I am."

Catfish gave a start and took a step back. "Damn. How'd you get so close without me seein' or hearin'?"

He quickly pressed the muzzle of his pistol to the back of Winona's head. "No tricks now."

Nate smiled at his wife. He admired how she held her head high, her chin raised defiantly. "I can't leave you alone for two minutes without you getting into trouble."

Catfish's brow knit in perplexity. "What kind of man are you? How can you joke at a time like this? Don't you realize what's at stake?"

"Where are your three friends?" Nate asked. Suddenly Winona started blinking. She blinked fast, stopped, and blinked fast again. Nate counted the blinks. Five each time. He understood. There were five of them, not four. He nodded at her. "Have I told you lately that you are the best wife any man could ever have?"

"Mountain man, you are damned peculiar," Catfish snapped. "Now I want you to drop your rifle and shed those pistols, and I want you to do it nice and slow."

Still gazing at Winona, Nate said, "You look tired. Why don't you lie down and rest?"

"What the hell?" Catfish said.

Winona dropped onto her side. In the same instant, Nate drew his pistol, cocking the hammer as he cleared his belt. Catfish, caught flat-footed, tried to raise his own pistol, but Nate was faster. His flintlock boomed and the heavy ball cored Catfish smack in the center of his forehead.

Behind Nate the underbrush crackled and out of it bounded a bucktoothed stripling who screamed, "Catfish! Catfish! Catfish!" He stopped and jerked his rifle up, but Nate already had his Hawken level. He fired at a range of no more than ten feet and blew the top of the young man's head off.

Winona keened a warning through her gag.

Nate whirled. Three more were rushing from the forest on the south side of the road. One was almost as big as him. Another wore buckskins. The third had a pockmarked face and was aiming a rifle. Nate dived as the rifle went off. Rolling as he hit, he drew his other pistol. The big man and the slave hunter in buckskins had ducked back under cover but the man with the pockmarked face was rushing him and unlimbering a pistol as he charged.

"I'll kill you, you bastard!"

Nate fired.

Pockmark reacted as if he had been punched in the chest. He lurched to a stop and half turned, a hand pressed to the hole in his sternum. He gaped down at himself in astonishment, bleated, "This can't be!" and died.

Winona rolled toward Nate. She knew he would not leave her there, and so long as they were in the open, they were, as the whites would say, sitting ducks.

A rifle cracked and a dirt geyser erupted a whisker's width from Nate's head. Heaving into a crouch, he ran to Winona and bent to scoop her into his arms. As he did, another rifle spoke, and this time a searing pain flared across his upper back. He had been hit, but he didn't let it stop him. Staying low, weaving madly, he made it to the north side of the road and plunged in among the trees. He managed a dozen strides before shock and weakness brought him to his knees. Gently, he lowered Winona and doubled over.

Winona had felt his body jar with the impact. Frantic with worry, she tried to spit the gag out of her mouth, but it was jammed deep.

"Let me," Nate said, and pulled the gag out.

"How bad is it?" Winona immediately asked.

"Give me a minute and I'll be back on my feet." Nate twisted around. There was no sign of the last two slave hunters. He had dropped his rifle out on the road when he picked up Winona, but he still had his pistols. Both were spent and he began to reload.

"Cut me loose," Winona urged, turning so her back was to him. A slash of the bowie was all it took to free her wrists, another to free her ankles. She sat up, cast the rope from her, and grabbed Nate's other pistol. "I'll reload this one."

"Samuel and his family?"

"In shackles. They were left with the horses." Winona pointed. "Not far that way."

"Shackles? Hell." Nate's fingers wouldn't quite work as they should. He got his powder horn open but it took some doing.

Winona rose. "Let me have a look at you." She moved around behind him and examined the wound. The ball had dug a furrow from his right shoulder to his left. It wasn't deep or life-threatening, but he would have another scar to add to his collection. "You'll live."

Nate kept glancing at the road. "Where are they? Why aren't they doing anything?"

"You killed three of them. They are being careful."

"Listen."

A horse whinnied. Hooves thudded and two riders burst from the vegetation and raced to the east, both bent low over their mounts.

"They're leaving!" Winona exclaimed in some amazement.

Nate couldn't believe it, either. Then again, they had seen their three friends slain, and maybe they reckoned they would share the same fate. Heaving upright, he went to the road. The pair hadn't stopped, and were almost to the bend. "I'll be damned."

Winona came up beside him. "I will load your rifle and we will go free the Worths."

"Who had the key to their shackles?"

"That one," Winona said, pointing at Catfish.

After freeing the Worths, Winona applied a salve to Nate's wound that relieved most of the pain. They stripped the dead slave hunters of weapons and gave them to the Worths. They also gave the Worths the three horses, with the saddles and bridles.

Patting his new rifle, Samuel summed up his family's feelings by saying, "We can't ever thank you enough for what you've done. We're free now. Truly and really free."

By the next morning they were on their way again.

Two weeks later the Kings and the Worths crossed the Mississippi River on a ferry.

Five days after they crossed, seven hard-faced men took the same ferry. Their lanky leader wore buckskins and carried a fine Kentucky rifle.

To be continued . . .

Look for *Wilderness #59: Only the Strong* in March 2009!

Author's Note

Nate King mentions the black man who lived with the Crows several times in his journal. His claim is corroborated by other sources. But there is some controversy as to the man's identity.

Some accounts say he was York, William Clark's slave. After the Lewis and Clark expedition returned, York asked to be set free. Clark said no, so York fled to the wilderness and lived with the Crows the remainder of his days.

Others would have it that the black man was Edward Rose, a renegade. Rose was known to have been in the West during the same period.

But since the black man living with the Crows told Nate King, Zenas Leonard, and others that he was, in fact, York, the author has seen fit to take him at his word.

John D. Nesbitt

"John Nesbitt knows working cowboys and ranch life well enough for you to chew the dirt with his characters." —*True West*

FIRST TIME IN PRINT!

Will Dryden picked the wrong time to ride onto the Redstone Ranch. He was looking for a job...and a missing man. But one of the Redstone's hands was just found killed, so tensions are riding high and not everyone's eager to welcome a stranger. The more questions Dryden asks, the more twisted everything seems, and the more certain he is that someone's got something to hide. Something worth killing for. Dryden just has to make sure he doesn't catch a bullet before he finds out what's behind all the...

TROUBLE AT THE REDSTONE

ISBN 13: 978-0-8439-6055-6

ROBERT J. CONLEY

FIRST TIME IN PRINT!

NO NEED FOR A GUNFIGHTER

"One of the most underrated and overlooked writers of our time, as well as the most skilled."
—Don Coldsmith, Author of the Spanish Bit Saga

BARJACK VS...EVERYBODY!

The town of Asininity didn't think they needed a tough-as-nails former gunfighter for a lawman anymore, so they tried—as nicely as they could—to fire Barjack. But Barjack likes the job, and he's not about to move on. With the dirt he knows about some pretty influential folks, there's no way he's leaving until he's damn good and ready. So it looks like it's the town versus the marshal in a fight to the finish... and neither side is going to play by the rules!

Conley is "in the ranks of N. Scott Momaday, Louise Erdrich, James Welch or W. P. Kinsella."
—*The Fort Worth Star-Telegram*

ISBN 13: 978-0-8439-6077-8

FIRST TIME IN PRINT!

OUTLAWS

PAUL BAGDON

Spur Award Finalist and Author of
Deserter and *Bronc Man*

Pound Taylor has just escaped from jail—and the hangman's noose—and he's eager to get back on the outlaw trail. For his gang he chooses his former cell-mate and the father and brothers of his old partner, Zeb Stone. Pound wants to do things right, with lots of planning and minimum gunplay, but the Stone boys figure they can shoot first and worry about the repercussions later. Sure enough, that's just what they do—and they kill a man in the process. With the law breathing down their necks and the whole gang at one another's throats, Pound can see that hangman's noose getting closer all the time. Unless his friends kill him first!

ISBN 13: 978-0-8439-6073-0